Modred lunged, too near to be stopped: his hand hit a control and there was a sound of hydraulics forward before Lance reached past Gawain and Percy and Lynn who pinned Modred to the counter. Lance hauled Modred out and swung him about and hit him hard. Modred hit the floor and slid over under the edge of Gawain's vacant seat, lying sprawled and limp.

Our lock was open. Modred had opened us up. The realization got through to Dela and she flew across the deck. "Close it—for God's sake close it," Dela cried, and I just stood there with my hands to my mouth because it was clear it was not happening.

"It's not working," Lynn said. "Lady Dela, there's something in the doorway...."

DAW

DAW Science-Fiction by
Hugo Award Winner
C. J. CHERRYH

PORT
ETERNITY

C. J. Cherryh

DAW BOOKS, INC.
DONALD A. WOLLHEIM, PUBLISHER

1633 Broadway, New York, NY 10019

DAW Book Collectors No. 500.

All quotations are from *Idylls of the King* by
Alfred Lord Tennyson.

FIRST PRINTING, OCTOBER 1982

3 4 5 6 7 8 9

PRINTED IN THE U.S.A.

. . . Fairy Queens have built the city, son;
. . . And as thou sayest it is enchanted, son,
For there is nothing in it as it seems
Saving the King; tho' some there be that hold
The King a shadow, and the city real. . . .

I

She was a beautiful ship, the *Maid of Astolat*, beautiful in
the way ships can be when cost means nothing, and money
certainly meant nothing except the comfort and the pleasure
of my lady Dela Kirn. I had seen the *Maid* from the outside,
but her crew had not, at least not since the day they boarded
her. She was beautiful outside and in, sleek, with raking lines
to her vanes which meant nothing at all in space, but pleased
the eye and let everyone know that this was no merchanter,
no; and inside, inside she was luxury and comfort, which I
appreciated too, more than I appreciated the engineering.
Where lady Dela went, I went, along with the other servants
lady Dela had for her personal comfort; but the *Maid* was
the best of the places Dela Kirn lived, and I was happiest
when she gave the order that packed up the household for the
winter season and took us up to station, for whatever destination pleased her.

Usually this move coincided with some new lover, and
some of these were good and some were not—more disagree-
able than pleasant, truth be told; but we managed, usually, to
enjoy ourselves by avoiding them at their worst. Often
enough the *Maid* had no really binding course, more duration
than destination. She just set out and toured this station and
another, and because Dela loved to travel, and grew bored

with this and that climate, we were a great deal on the move.

Dela Kirn, be it understood, was one of the Founders of Brahman, not that she herself had founded a world, but her predecessors had, so Dela Kirn inherited money and power and in short, whatever she had ever fancied to have or do.

My name is Elaine, which amused my lady Dela, who gave the name to me. I have a number on my right hand, very tiny and tasteful, in blue; and the same number on my shoulder, 68767-876-998, which I *am*, if anyone asked, and not Elaine. *Elaine* was Dela Kirn's amusement. I was *made* 68767-876-998. *Born* isn't the right word, being what I am, which is a distinction I don't fully understand, only that my beginning was in a way different than birth, and that I was planned. I've never had any other name than Elaine, I think, because before Dela I have no clear memory where I was, except that it was nowhere—one of the farms. On the farms they lock you up and you spend a lot of time doing repeat work and a lot of time exercising and a lot of time under deepteach or just blanked, and none if it is pleasant to think back on. When I have nightmares they tend to be of that, of being locked up alone, with just my own mind for company.

They worked over my genes in planning me, me, 68767-876-998, so that I'm beautiful and intelligent, which isn't vanity to say, because I had nothing at all to do with it. And probably there are hundreds of me, because I was a successful combination, and a lot aren't. I cost my lady a lot of money, like the *Maid*, but then, she wouldn't have wanted me if I hadn't.

And Lancelot and Vivien were beautiful too, which they were made to be . . . Dela gave them their names from the same source she got mine, having this fancy for an old poem-tape. I knew. I had heard it. The story made me sad, especially since that Elaine, the lily maid, died very young. I knew of course that I would too, which happens to our type . . . they take us when we get a little beyond forty and put us down, unless we have learned by then to be very clever or unless we have somehow become very important, which few of us do.—But they made us on tape, feeding knowledge into our heads by that means, while they grew our bodies, so I suppose they have the right to do that, like throwing out tape when it gets worn—or when we wear out, beyond use.

Lance—for him I felt sorriest of all when I first heard the

tape, because of what he was and because of the story too, that it came out just as badly for him. It was a terrible story, and a grand one at the same time. I heard it over and over again, whenever I had the chance, loving it, because in a way it was me, a me I would never be, except in my dreams. Only I never wanted to give it to Lance to hear, or even to Viv, because their part in it was crueler than mine; and somehow I was afraid it might come true, even if we have no love the way born-men do.

Dying—that, of course, we do, all of us. But what it was to love . . . I only dreamed.

I was still young, having served my lady Dela just five years. Vivien was older; and so was Lance, who was trained for other things than keeping the household in order, I may add, and very handsome, more than any of Dela's other lovers that she had for other reasons. Dela was good to Lance when she was between lovers, and as far as we could love, I think Lance loved her very much. He had to. That was what *his* taped psych-set made him good for, and mostly it was what he thought about, besides being beautiful. He was older than any of us, being thirty-six—and forty frightened him.

I was, precisely, twenty-one, after five years' service; because really my mind was better than the training they put into it—and I was sold out at sixteen, finished two years younger than most leave the farms. I read; I wrote; I sang; I knew how to dress and how to do my lady's hair and how to make love and do simplest math, all of which recommended me, I suppose. But mostly I was innocent, which pleased my lady Dela. She liked the look of me, she would say, holding my face in her two hands and smiling. I have chestnut hair and greenish eyes, and I blush quickly, which would make her laugh; besides that I have, she would say, a face like in the old romance, my eyes being very large for my face and my skin decidedly pale. I have a romantical sad look—not that I am sad a great deal of the time, but I have the look. So I was Elaine, the lily maid, like the ship. Elaine loved Lancelot and died for love, Elaine my namesake in the poem, but love was very far from me.

Actually, if I had something to make me melancholy, it was that I had that name which meant dying young, and I had been out of the farms so short a time that death, however romantical, hardly appealed to me. I had never thought much about death before that tape—but I did think of it afterward.

Vivien—Vivien now: she was different, all sharpness and wit, and that was *her* function, not being beautiful, although she was, in a dark and elegant fashion. The Vivien of the story was a cold and intelligent woman; and so was ours, who managed the accounts and all the things that Dela found too tedious, the really complicated things. Age had no terror for Vivien—she was sure to go on past forty: without *her*, my lady Dela would hardly have known what to do about her taxes.

Mostly Viv kept to herself. She was of course older, but she looked down not just on me, but on Lance—which she had a right to do, being the most likely of us all to be given rejuv and to live as long as Dela herself. Viv did sleep with us in the servants' quarters, and she talked to us without spite, but she was not like us. I bored her; and Landce did, entirely, because Viv had no sex drive at all and made no sense of Lance. Attractive and elegant as she was, she got all her pleasure from her account-keeping and from organizing things and telling us what to do, which is as good a way to get pleasure as any other, I suppose, if it works, which it seemed to do for Vivien.

Then there was the crew, who were like us all, made for what they did. Their pleasures were mostly of Vivien's sort—taking care of the ship and seeing that everything aboard was in order. Only sometimes they did have sex when the *Maid* was in dock, at least three of them, because there was nothing else for them to do. They lived all their lives waiting on Dela's whim to travel.

The men were Percivale, Gawain, and Modred. Modred was a joke of kinds, because he was one of the really cold ones who mostly cared for his computers and his machines; and there was Lynette, who was the other pilot besides Gawain. None of them could make anyone pregnant and Lynette couldn't get pregnant, so it was all safe enough, whatever they did; but they had that kind of psych-set that made them go off sex the moment they were set on duty. The moment the ship activated, the ship became mistress to all of them: they served the *Maid* in a kind of perpetual chastity in flight, except a few times when my lady had guests aboard and lent them out.

That was the way we lived.

On this particular voyage there was just one guest, and my lady Dela was busy with him from the time we all came aboard. He was her favorite kind of lover, very rich and better still—young. He had not yet gone into rejuv; was golden and blond and very serious. His name was Griffin, and it might have been one of Dela's own conceits, but it really was his name. It meant a kind of beast which was neither one thing nor the other, and that was very much like Griffin. He read a great deal and had a hand in everything; he spent a lot of his off time enjoying tape dramas, to my great delight . . . for with that store of them which had come aboard the *Maid* because of him, I was going to have a great many of them to spend time with, as I had had constantly during the time he had been at the country estates at Brahmani Dali. Born-man dramas were a kind of deepteach I dearly loved, stories where you could just stretch out and let your mind go, and *be* those people. (But several of his tapes I had not liked at all, and they gave me nightmares: This was also Griffin. They were about hurting people, and about wars, and I hated that, but there never was a way to tell what kind of stories they were when I was sneaking them out of library, no way at all to tell what I was going to get until I took the drug and turned the machine on, and then, of course, it was too late to back out.) All of this was Griffin, who came from neighboring Sita, and who visited for business and stayed for pleasure. He surprised us at first by staying longer than a week, and then a month, and four, and lastly by getting invited to the *Maid*. He was, truth be known, half Dela's real age, although she never looked the difference . . . she was seventy, and looked thirty, because Dela hated the thought of getting old, and started her rejuv at that age, for vanity's sake, and also I think because she had no desire for children, which holds most born-men off it another decade. At thirty-odd Griffin had not yet needed it, although he was getting to that stage when he might soon think of it. He attended on Dela. He slept with no one else; his vices were secret and invisible— austere by comparison to some of Dela's companions. By the stories Griffin liked, I suspected he was one of those who didn't mind being hurt, and my lady was certainly capable of obliging him.

Dela herself. Dela was, as I say, thirtyish looking, though over twice that, and she dyed the silver that rejuv made of her hair, so that it was palest blonde and she wore it in great beautiful braids. She was elegant, she was pink and gold and quite, quite small. She never liked figures and accounting; but she loved planning things and having things built. She built four cities on Brahman, with all their parks and shops, and owned them. All the inside of the *Maid* was Dela's planning, down to the light fixtures, and the sheets on the beds. She had built the *Maid* a long time ago—the *Maid* was getting old inside, just like Dela (but still beautiful) and she was something worth seeing, though few ever did. She was a fairytale; and special to Dela. Deep inside Dela I think there was something that hated life as it was, and hated her expensive safety, and the guards and the precautions that were all about her on Brahman. She hated these things and loved the stories until she began to shape them about her—and shaping them, she shaped the *Maid*.

I thought by that strange fancy I could understand Dela, who lived stories that were long ago and only maybe so, whose life came down to tapes, just like mine.

Tapes and new lovers. Like Lance, she was desperately frightened of getting old. So I always knew how to please her, which was to make her believe she was young. When Dela was happy she could be kind and thoughtful; but when things went badly, they went badly for all of us, and we mourned her lost lovers with earnest grief—all of us, that is, except Lance, whose psych-set drove him inevitably to comfort her, so Lance always had the worst of it. If there was ever a face that life *made* sad—Dela always favored the storybook looks—it was surely Lance's, beautiful as he was; and somehow he had gotten caught in it all unawares, because she had never given him the old story tapes I had heard. I always thought he would have understood that other Lancelot, who lost whenever he seemed to win.

Maybe Dela was a little crazy. Some of her peers said so, in my hearing, when I was making myself a part of the furniture. It is true that we lived in a kind of dream, who lived with Dela Kirn; but only those who entered the *Maid* ever saw the heart of it, the real depth of her fancy. The ship was decorated in a strange mix of old fables and shipboard modern, with swords, real swords and hand-stitched banners fixed on the walls, and old-looking beams masking the structural joinings, and lamps that mimicked live flame in some of the rooms like the beautiful dining hall or her own private compartments. And those who became her lovers and played her game for a while—they seemed to enjoy it.

It struck me increasingly strange, me, who had nothing of property, and was instead owned and made, that for Dela Kirn who could buy thousands of my kind and even have us made to order . . . the greatest joy in her life was to pretend. All my existence was pretense, the pretense of the tapes which fed into my skull what my makers and my owner wanted me to know and believe; and until I was sold to Dela and until I saw Dela's secret fancies, I thought that the difference between us and born-men was that born-men lead real lives, and see what really is, and that this was the power born-men have over the likes of us. But all Dela wanted with all her power was to unmake what was, and to shape what the story tapes told her until she lived and moved in it. So then I was no longer sure what was true and what was false, or what was best in living, to be me, or to be Dela Kirn.

Until the end, of course, when they would put me down because I had no more usefulness, while Dela went on and on living on rejuv, which our kind almost never got. Seventy. I could not, from twenty-one, imagine seventy. She had already lived nearly twice as long as I ever could, and she had seen more and done more, living all of it, and not having the first fifteen years on tape.

Maybe, I thought, in seventy years she had worn out what there was to know; and that might be why she turned to her fables.

Or she was mad.

If one has most of the wealth of a world at one's disposal, if one has built whole cities and filled them with people and gotten bored with them, one can be mad, I suppose, and not be put down for it . . . especially if one owns the hospitals and the labs. And while far away there was a government which sent warnings to Dela Kirn, she laughed them off as she did most unpleasant things and said that they would have to come and do something about it, but that they were busy doing other things, and that they needed Brahman's good will. About such things I hardly know, but it did seem to work that way. No one came from the government but one angry man, and a little time in Dela's country house at Brahmani Dali under our care, and some promises of philanthropy, sent him back happier than he had come.

This much I understood of it, that Dela had bought her way out of that problem as she had bought off other people who stood in her way; and if ever Dela could not buy her way through a difficulty, then she threatened and frightened people with her money and what it could do. If Dela felt anything about such contests, I think it was pleasure, after it was all over—pleasure at the first, and then a consuming melancholy, as if winning had not been enough for her.

But the *Maid* was her true pleasure, and her real life, and she only brought her favorite lovers to it.

So she brought Griffin . . . all gaiety, all happiness as we hurried about the *Maid*'s rich corridors settling everyone in our parting from Brahmani Station—but there was a foreboding about it all which my lady understood and perhaps Griffin did not; it was months that she would love a man before she thought it enough to bring him to the *Maid*, and after that, it was all downhill, and she had no more to give him. The dream would end for him, because no one could live in Dela's story forever.

Only we, Elaine and Lancelot and Vivien; and Percy and Wayne and Modred . . . we were always there when it ended; and Lance would be hurt as he always was; and I would comfort him—but he never loved me . . . he was fixed on Dela.

So we set off on holiday, to play out the old game and to revel while we could, and to make Dela happy a time, which was why we existed at all.

Then ran across her memory the strange rhyme
Of bygone Merlin, "Where is he who knows?
From the great deep to the great deep he goes."

II

Griffin, as I say, was one of the strange ones my lady Dela picked up from time to time, not easy to fix which of his several natures was the real one, no. I had found him frightening from the start, truth be told. He didn't laugh often, but much when he did, and he could be mortally stubborn and provoke Dela to rages which came down on all of us and darkened the house at Brahmani Dali for days. He interfered with Dela's business and talked to Vivien about the books, which ordinarily Dela would never allow—but Griffin did, and had his way about it, amid storms in the country house which would have disposed of less appealing lovers. He wound himself in tighter and tighter with my lady's business, and that disturbed us all.

He was an athletic sort, who looked rather more like one of us than he did like a born-man; but then, they play games even with born-man genes when women are rich, and Griffin certainly came from wealthy beginnings. Like Lance, Griffin seemed to fill whatever room he was in. He was very tall and slim in the hips and wide in the shoulders . . . and he had an interesting, strong-boned face—not so fine as Lance, who was dark-haired and handsome and had meltingly dark eyes; but Griffin was bronzed and blond like one of the knights in the storybook tape. That answered, physically, why Dela had been attracted at the outset.

But Griffin was not, like most of her previous lovers,

13

empty-headed; and he had not gotten pretty by spending all his time taking care of that beautiful body. He was just that way, which left the rest of his time to be doing something else—and in Griffin's case, that something else was meddling with Dela's business or lying lost in the tapes. He was one of the few men I ever did know who looked merely asleep under the tapes, and not lackwitted: Griffin did not know how to be ungraceful, I think it was muscle. He just did not collapse when he slept the deepsleep. And when he was awake, he was imposing. He tended to stare through the likes of me, or at very most remembered and thanked me for doing some small extra service for him—a courtesy far greater than I had gotten from most of my lady's associations, and at the same time, far less, because he could still look through me while he was thanking me. He never bedded with me, and he was the first of Dela's lovers who had never done that. He stayed to Dela. That fact upset me at first, but he bedded with none of the estate servants male or female either, so I understood it was not my failing: he simply wanted Dela, uniquely and uninterrupted by others—quite, quite different from the usual. I saw them together, matched, blond and blonde, storybook knight and storybook lady, a man full of ideas, a man my lady let into more than the bedchamber. He was change; and he frightened us in strange and subtle ways.

What, we wondered, when she should tire of him?

We had set out from station that morning, and Dela was taking a nap, because we had been up too many hours getting up from the world and getting settled in, and we had gone through a time change. We were, of course, under acceleration and moving a little cautiously when we walked, but nothing uncomfortable: the *Maid* rarely hurried. Griffin was still up and about, typical of the man, to be meddling with charts and tapes and comp in his cabin; and he wanted a little of my lady's imported brandy. I brought it to his cabin, which was next to Dela's own, and since he had not dismissed me I stood there while he sipped the brandy and fussed with his papers.

This time? I wondered. It would spoil all my reckonings of him if he asked me to bed with him now. I stood thinking about it, watching his broad back, no little distressed, thinking of all those tapes he listened to, about murdering and pain. He was altogether imposing under those circumstances. Dela was abed, drugged down; perhaps he felt he needed someone. A lot of people get nervous before jump. I waited. I blanked, finally, went null as my knees locked up, and I was in some pain; blinked alert as he stood up and looked down at me.

"I'm sorry," was all he said. "Go. Go on. That's all."

"Thank you, sir," I said, wondering now if it would have pleased him had I been forward with him: some expected that. I looked back from the doorway. But Griffin had snugged down on the bed on his belly, head on his arms, and looked genuinely content enough: the brandy seemed to have had its effect. So he was happy; Dela would be. That was all I wanted. I went back and took the empty glass, set it on the tray, and left.

It might not be, I was thinking then, so bad a voyage, Griffin simply remaining Griffin: some men changed aboard, becoming bizarre in their fancies and their demands, but he did not. I diverted myself through the library, a simple jog from the corridor that joined his and Dela's cabin and the outer hall, into the library/deepsleep lab, with its double couch. A touch of a button, the unsealing of a clear-faced cabinet, neat tucking of a tape cassette into my coveralls pocket and off and out the other door, into the same hall and out into the main corridor. Dela never minded, but then, Dela had whims: I kept my borrowings neat and quiet.

The galley then, on lowermost level, and up again to our own quarters, midway in the ship, very nice, very comfortable, after the fashion of things aboard the *Maid*. Deep, fine beds, the finest sheets, fine as Dela's own—she never scanted us. Beautiful thick carpet, all the colors rust and brown and cream, a fine curved couch wrapped all the way around the corner, one level behind the other, with multiple deepstudy outlets, and the screens above, on the ceiling. Lance was there, not deepstudying, just sitting on the couch, arms on his knees, looking downhearted and tragic as he usually did at such settings-forth. I had had some thought of using my tapes; I gave it up, and sat down by Lance and took his hand in my lap and simply went into blank again. For us too, it had been too many time changes, and it would be better for Lance when he was rested.

Vivien came in, from attending whatever business had occupied her with the station and the undocking, accounts and charges all squared, presumably. Not the least drooping, not a sleekly chignoned hair mussed, but Viv was on our schedule: she had a brittleness to her movements, all the same. And came Percy and Lynette, of the crew, who were on ship's time and who looked like business as they usually did when we saw them. Percy was a youngish man with red hair and a delightful beard, all very close and delicately trimmed, his great vanity. And Lynn, Lynn was a flat and ethereal sort with an aquiline nose and freckles that had never seen much of any sun, brown hair trimmed as close as Percy's.

"What sort have we got this trip?" Percy asked, reclining on the nearest bed, his booted ankles crossed. He propped himself up sidelong on his elbow. This was our haven, this room. We could say what we liked with no one listening, so it was safe for him to ask. Lynette had settled sidelong the other way, leaning against him, not flirting, but because we all like touching when we relax, which is the way we are, sexed or not. Percy and Lynn, being crew, and busy all this while, had not yet met Griffin.

I shrugged. That was the kind of impression I had to give about Griffin, that I didn't have a clear impression, even after all this time. We had gotten used to him down at Brahmani Dali, as much as one could get used to Griffin—which meant we accepted that he would be up to something constantly, and alternately upsetting my lady and pleasing her.

"I don't like him," Lance said suddenly. Four months of silence, and: "I don't like him." He had never said that before, not even with some of my lady's absolute worst, who had abused him and any others of us accessible. "I wish she would get rid of him."

That frankness upset me. It was one thing to think it, but it was another to say it out like that, even here.

"This one," said Vivien, "this one is different than the others. I think she might *marry* this one."

"No," I exclaimed, and put my hand over my mouth, guilty as Lance.

"Why else does she have me going over her accounts and letting him into them, and why does she have spies going over *his?* She said once she might marry him. I don't think it was a joke. I think she's really thinking about it. It has to do with that government business last year. This Griffin's family has influence. And the worlds, Brahman and Sita—position for a natural alliance. The government has other concerns at the moment, can't afford prolonged trouble in this direction. And besides—she seems to enjoy him."

Viv looked satisfied. *Her* position wasn't threatened. No one said anything for a while. This move seemed then to have monetary reasons behind it, which we understood: everything my lady did seriously tended to have such reasons in it, so this frightened me more and more. "He's not so bad," I said, not that I really believed it, but Lance was beside me and his hand was sweating in mine. "And she'll get cooler toward him someday. If he stays—it'll still happen that way, won't it? And he's never done anything to any of us, not like that Robert she took up with."

There was a general muttering, a reflexive jerk of Lance's hand. Robert had been the worst.

"Maybe she'll get some favor out of him or his family," Lynette said, "and then it'll be like the others."

"But she talked about marrying," Vivien persisted, unstoppable. "And she's never considered that. Ever. Griffin's intelligent, she says. Someone who could run things in years to come. She's never talked like that about the others. He's *young*."

More silence and heavier, even from Percy and Lynette, who were generally not bothered with estate finances and problems of that sort. After all, if another owner came into the picture, if Griffin began to involve himself permanently and changed Dela's way of operating—then the *Maid* might not go on making such trips as she did now. So the crew faced uncertainties too.

The *Maid* might—the thought came washing over me— might even be *sold*, and so might we all, being part of a fancy Dela might tire of if she changed her life and stopped taking lovers. Being sold was . . . I could not imagine it. I had heard dread whispers that it meant being taken back into the labs for retraining, and that meant they took your mind apart. It was effectively like dying. I didn't say that aloud. We had enough troubles, all of us. And Lance . . . he was old for retraining. Lance could be put down.

I was never inclined to sudden panics, but I had one. I sat

there and blanked, and when I came out of it, Lance was tugging at my hand to shake me out of it.

"Elaine?" he said.

I clenched his hand in mine and said nothing.

"We're going to make jump sooner than usual," Lynn said. "She's told us to keep up acceleration all the way. It has to do with *him,* maybe. Ask Wayne and Modred about particulars: but it's Delhi."

The regional capital. The kind of place her ladyship had stayed out of, with her wealth which she had no desire thus far to flaunt near the government.

"Griffin has property on Delhi," Vivien said.

"What kind?" I asked, heart pounding, because I had heard of establishments on Delhi where a lot of our kind came from. Percivale was one of Delhi's breeding, so he said; and I knew that Modred was.

"Farms," Vivien said tautly. "And training centers. Labs. They've been talking about taking an interest in that. In shifting assets—Griffin's wealth and our lady's can pull hard weight in Delhi Council if they start playing games with banks. Those kind of maneuvers . . . Griffin can do. All he has to do is free up some currency. His farms there—"

Then they all seemed to think of selling and being sold, and Percy blanked, and Lynn too, for a moment, like two statues reclining there.

"I think we should get some sleep," Vivien said, with a stretch of her back. She had spent all *she* had to say, and in our matters, that was as far as Vivien's interest went. She got up and left. Sleep seemed a good idea, because there was certainly nothing pleasant to think of awake. We moved to our beds, all of which were close together, and began to get undressed. Only Lance still sat there, and I felt sorry for him. They psych-set me so that I can't stand to see someone suffering. Born-men feel; we react; so the difference runs. And Lance was reacting to everything, and especially to this most frightening of the lady's affairs. I think maybe he would rather have had Robert aboard again. Any of them. It had already been hard on him, this involvement with Griffin, lasting now for four months and promising to go on *long*—but *marry* him . . . and all this maneuvering, this trip to Delhi which seemed to make it all more and more like the truth. . . . All this had surely struck poor Lance to the gut.

He wasn't blanked, and it would have been healthier if he were. He just sat there like he was bleeding inside.

"Come on," I said, walking back over to tug at his hand. "I want you"—which was a lie. I was tired, but it was his psych-set, and it gave him something to react to that would take his mind off Dela and off his own future at least for the moment. He undressed and we got between the sheets. He made love to me . . . he *was* good. What handsome blond Griffin was like I had no idea, but if it were me, or if I were lady Dela, I would have preferred Lance, who was very beautiful and who did sex very well and with endless invention, which was what he was made for.

Only his eyes were sadder than ever and he was not, this time, as good as he could be. His body reacted to his psych-set; and that was that, tired or not, up to reasonable limits. But there were times when Lance was *there* and times when he was not, and this time he was not. Worry, like everything else, every other disturbance in his patterns, he channelled into his psych-set outlet the way he was healthily supposed to, so he was not breaking down and he didn't panic, but it was as close to panic as I had ever seen him.

I held him close for a long time afterward and tried to keep his mind on me—which it had never been, all the while—because I *liked* him, in a different way than I liked anyone else. I would have called it love, but love—was for the likes of the lady Dela, who could fall into and out of grand and glorious passions, sighing and suffering and flying into rages. We just blank when we're upset. The least anguish of an emotional sort turns us off like a light going out unless we're directly ordered to stay around, or unless we're occupied about some duty. We have better sense than to cause ourselves such pains, and we have better manners than to tease one another too seriously—which, besides, would be interfering with Dela's property, and rather like vandalism, which we could not do either.

Pilferage now . . . borrowing . . . that we could do. I got up and got the tape I had pilfered out of the library and set the hookups over by the couch for Lance and me, figuring that he needed an escape just now. He wanted only to lie there staring at the ceiling, but I took him by the hand and pulled at him until he stirred out of bed and came; and then he put the sensors on himself and took the drug gladly

enough when I gave it to him. I got a blanket and my own
rigging fixed, drugged out and settled in, hoping for something good.

It was a story tape: I had thought so from where I pilfered
it; but it was one of *those*, one of Griffin's, that could almost
kill you with fright. I knew when I was still sliding into it
what it was going to be, and I tried to open my mouth to yell
out to Percy or someone to help, get it off us, pull us out of
it, but I must have been too far gone. No one came.

Only the story got better. Lance and I were in it together,
and while it was more bloody than I liked, I found myself enjoying it after all. That was it: once you give your mind to
one of these things, especially if you're down, that means the
drugs have got your threshold flat and you're locked into the
tape, so that you'll agree to whatever happens. I lived it.
Lance did, to whatever degree he could, according to his own
pre-programming. Probably he was what I was, which was a
hero, and very strong and extraordinarily brave and angry.
Griffin had a passion for such stories, of angry men. For a
little while I could handle anything at all: I was a born-man;
and I fought a great deal and sometimes made love to a very
beautiful blonde lady who reminded me of Dela. Lance
would have loved *that*. And I'll bet the men he fought were
all Griffin; but for me they were Robert, that I killed a dozen
times and enjoyed it more thoroughly than I liked to think
about when I finally woke out of it.

But when I did wake up I knew for sure it was not the
kind of tape that we were ever supposed to have, not at all,
because it was violent, and bloody, and all my psych-sets
were disturbed. Lance was that way about it too, and avoided
my eyes and seemed to be thinking about something. So I figured I had better get this one back into that library before it
was missed.

We *can* deceive, at least I could, and Lance could, and
probably all of us. Vivien and Lynette and Modred were too
cold to play games . . . or to talk much with born-men, a
silence which was deception of another kind, when they had
reason to use it. At least that trio wouldn't get up and sneak
about some project for their own personal pleasure.

But Modred, now. . . .

Modred was the one I went to when I wanted a tape back

in the library undetected, a ride up in the lift toward the bow, up to the bridge where duties were still going on. No one suspected Modred of nonsense like tape-pilfering; and he *would* take my orders, because the operational crew maintained the library and were always pulling references to this and that through the computer. If I wanted a tape for my own use for a while, it was nothing for him to spin a tape through and record it, and then do things with the records of its use. It was even less for him to play with the records and drop a tape into the chute for the automated sorting to whisk back to its slot in the rack back in library. He could do that and never miss a beat in what else he was doing, and I think he really preferred the more complicated larcenies: they were problems, and this was not.

Modred and Gawain. Wayne, we called the one, for short: he had long brown hair, and was very handsome—but he was all business whenever I would see him, given to working himself very hard. He was the mainday pilot, as Lynn ran things on alterday shift, and Percy was alterday comp. Gawain had a work compulsion, which tended to make Gawain lose weight when we were on long trips, but he really enjoyed what he did, and smiled a lot when he was working. Me, with my psych-set to worry about other's pain, I always carried him his dinners when he forgot them and when I happened to be awake on the same schedule; and I did the same for Modred, who shared his shift and also worked too much and got too thin, but who never showed exuberance about it. Modred was the only one but me whose name we never shortened to something sensible, because when we did it came out Dread, and that was just too much like him to be clever. Modred had a beard as black as Percy's was red, one of those jawline-following thin ones, but very heavy despite how close he cut it, and while Gawain let his hair go down to his shoulders for vanity's sake, Modred had his cut very short—Lynn and Percy played barber, among other skills— and he cut it square across his brow, which made his dark eyes very sinister. That was why my lady Dela named him Modred, and I think why she bought him, because she was fascinated by dangerous-looking men. Even born-men moved out of Modred's way, and that was a useful thing with some of the guests Dela had had. Not that Modred would *hurt* anyone, being like us, psych-set against it, but he looked like he would, and people reacted to that. Actually, he seemed to enjoy doing me small favors I asked, and getting small attentions from me and from Lynn when she was in the mood. Mostly that grim face—handsome, because my lady would not have had him about otherwise—seemed to me to conceal a very blank sort, who did his duty, who thought and calculated constantly, and who liked, like the rest of us, to sleep close at night, with someone close enough to let him feel companied. Vivien avoided sleeping next to him, somewhat scared of him, truth be told—and I always preferred Lance. So mostly Modred, really sexless, slept with his crewmates, who were also sexless during the voyages, and they kept each other company. Likely those four were neither concerned nor jealous about the freedom Lance and Viv and I had to come and go with my lady, to be in attendance on her, to share her luxuries, and in my case, to share her lovers—because they four were psych-fixed to the *Maid*, and when Modred or the others handled her controls, I think it was really like touching the body of a lover. It was a sort of grim joke, the stainless steel *Maid* and her crew doomed to love her with a chaste and forever devotion.

I preferred Lance.

But I flirted with Modred because it was pleasant. I always suspected he liked my touching him . . . at least that killer's face of his acquired a certain placidity like a pet being stroked by a familiar hand. He was not immune to sensation; it was just sex that was missing in him.

"Thank you," I whispered in his ear, leaning close, when he settled back into his place at the console, from disposing of the tape for me. I was not supposed to be on the bridge, any more than Modred was supposed to be doing things to the library records, but *supposed* was often a very lax word in my lady Dela's world: Dela cared nothing about laws or limitations in anyone. As long as the *Maid* served well as what she was, an abode of utmost luxury, and an extravagantly expensive toy, then what her living toys did in their off hours was of no concern. We could have held orgies on the bridge and abstracted the whole library to the crew quarters had we liked, and if my lady was in one of her relaxed moods, she would notice nothing.

There were, of course, other moods. Remembering those, we always kept the record purified.

"They'll be wanting you," Modred said in his flat way, staring at his screens to find out where things stood at the moment. Gawain was at the main console. I had my hands on Modred's shoulders and leaned to deposit a kiss on the side of his neck, which he took about like the touch of my hands, as something relaxingly pleasant. "I think my lady is awake."

He could do that, never missing the thread of the conversation when I teased him, which was the difference between him and Gawain or Percy, who at least grew bothered.

"I'll see to it," I said, and patted his shoulder. Actually Modred fascinated me because he *couldn't* be moved, and it was my function to move people. I hadn't seen him in months, and it was a new chance to try.

I had once tried more direct approaches, in the crew quarters. I think Modred wanted, with some dim curiosity, to do what others did, but it was only curiosity. "Let him alone," Lynn had said when she saw it, with a frown that meant business.

So you play the same game with him, I had thought then, but likewise Lynette was not one to cross lightly; and when it occurred to me that I might hurt someone my psych-set intervened and cooled me down at once. I confined myself after that to small games that Modred himself found pleasant.

"We're going to make jump in another hour," Gawain said from his post.

I wrinkled my nose. That meant getting my lady and the rest of us prepped with the drugs to endure jump. That was what she wanted, then. Jump always scared me, even drugged. It was the part of voyages that I hated.

And then: "*Modred*—" Gawain said in a plaintive voice I had never heard him use. It frightened me. Modred's reaction did, because he flung off my hand and reached for another board in a hurry, and alarms were going off, shrieking.

"Out!" he shouted, and Modred never shouted. I scrambled toward the exit, staggering as the whole ship heeled, and then vocal alarms were going, the *take-hold*, which means wherever you are, whatever is closest, regardless. I never made the door. I grabbed the nearest emergency securing and got the belt round me, while already the *Maid* was swinging in a roll so that we came under *G* like coming off a world.

"We're losing it," Gawain shouted into com. "We're losing it—Modred—"

"I don't know what it is," Modred yelled back. "Instruments . . . instruments are going crazy. . . ."

I looked up from my position crouched against the bulkhead, looked at the screens, and there was nothing but black on them. We were in the safe area of our own home star and with traffic around us. There was no way anything ought to be going wrong, but *G* was pulling us and making the lights all over the boards blink red, red, red.

Then it was as if whatever was holding us had just stopped existing, no jolt, but like sliding on oil, like a horrible falling where there *is* no falling.

And jump. Falling, falling, falling forever as we hurtled into subspace. I screamed and maybe even Modred did—I heard Gawain's voice for sure, and it became space and color. There was no ship, but naked chaos all around me, that stayed and stayed and stayed.

. . . and from them rose
A cry that shivered to the tingling stars,
And, as it were one voice, an agony
Of lamentation, like a wind that shrills
All night in a waste land, where no one comes,
Or hath come, since the making of the world.

III

I don't like to think of that time, and it was a long, long while before it dawned on me that I could move, and draw myself back from the void where I was. Things were all distorted. It seemed I could see through the hull, and through myself. Sometimes the chaos was red and sometimes the red became black and red spots crawled here and there like spiders. I cried, and there were other sounds that might be other voices, or the *Maid* herself still screaming.

Then like in the time before I left that white place where I was made, I had to have something to look at, to control the images, to sort truth from illusion, and I concentrated simply on getting my hand in front of my face. Knowing what it ought to look like, I could begin to make it out, bones and veins and muscles and skin. Not red. Not black. My own true color. I concentrated on it until it took the shape and texture it ought to have, and then I was able to see shadows of other things too, like the deck, and the rest of my own body lying there.

"Gawain," I cried, and by concentrating on shapes I could see the controls, and Gawain, who looked dead hanging in the straps; and Modred, who lay on the floor . . . his restraint had given way, as mine must have, and it should have broken my ribs, but it had not . . . there was, at least, no pain. Modred was trying to move too, like something inky writhing there on the deck, but I knew who it was, and I crawled across the floor which was neither warm nor cold nor rough nor smooth . . . I made it and got his hand, and hoped for help, because Modred was frightened by nothing, and if there was any of us who had a cold enough mind up here to be able to see what to do, I had most hope of Modred.

"Hung in the between," he said. "I think we're hung up in the between."

His voice did strange things in my head, echoed round and round as if my brains had been some vast room. For a moment I didn't want to look down, because there *was* a Down and we were still falling into it. Gawain had to get us out of this; that was all I could think of, and somehow Modred was pulling himself to his feet and heading in Gawain's direction. I scrambled up to follow him, and stood swaying with one foot on one side of a chasm and the other foot on the other side, stars between, the whole flowing like a river in born-men's Hell, all fire and glowing with the stars like brighter coals. *Don't move*, my brain kept telling my body, and I didn't for a moment. I stood there and shut my eyes.

But there is an advantage in being what we are, which is that wherever we are, that's what *is*, and we don't have such problems as some do, trying to relate it to anywhere else. I was upright. I set one foot out and insisted to feel what was under it, and after that I knew that I could walk. I moved after Modred, though the room kept shrinking and expanding insanely, and sometimes Gawain was very far away and sometimes just out of reach, but two-dimensional, so that he seemed pressed between two pieces of glass, and his beautiful hair hanging down at an unconscious angle seemed afire like the river of stars, streaming and flowing like light.

"Gawain!" Modred shouted, all distorted.

"Gawain!" I shouted too.

Gawain finally began to move, slow reaching of an arm which was at the moment two-dimensional and stretched all out of proportion. He tried to sit upright, and reached for the boards or what looked like an analogue of them in this distortion of senses, a puddle of lights which flowed and ran in swirling streams of fire.

He's there, I insisted to my rebel senses, and he began to be solid, within reach, as I knew he had to be. I grasped Modred's arm and reached for Gawain's, and Gawain twisted around and held onto both of us, painfully tight. "What you want to see, you *can* see," I said. "Don't imagine, Gawain. *Don't imagine.*"

He was there, all right. I could feel him heaving for breath, and I was breathing in the same hoarse gulps, and so was that third part of us, Modred.

"We've been malfunctioned into jump," Modred said, carefully, softly between gasps for breath. Voices distorted in my ears, and maybe in his too. "I think we're hung up somewhere in subspace and there's no knowing what happened back there. We could have dragged mass with us into this place. We could have dragged at the sun itself. I don't know. The instruments aren't making sense."

"Lady Dela," I said, thinking about her caught in this disaster, Dela, who was the reason for all of us existing at all.

"No drugs," Gawain murmured. "We're in this with no drugs."

That frightened me. We drug down to cope with the between of jump, that nowhere between here and there. But we were doing it without, if that was where we were . . . and like walking a tightrope across that abyss, the only hope was not to look down and not to lose our balance to it. One necessity at a time. "I'm going for lady Dela," I said.

"You'll get lost," Gawain protested, because the floors were still going in and out on us, turning reds and blacks and showing stars in the middle. "Don't. If we ripped something loose back there, if those corridors aren't sound. . . ."

"Use com." That was Modred, clearer headed than either of us. Modred passed me like a great black spider, and reached into the pool of lights, perhaps able to see them better because he knew what ought to be there. "Lady Dela," he said. "Lady Dela, this is Modred on the bridge. Do you hear me?"

"Modred!" a voice wailed back like crystal chimes. "Help!"

"Lady Dela!" I said. "Make up your mind to see . . . can you see? Look at something familiar until it makes sense."

"Help me," she cried.

"Do you see anything?" Gawain asked her. "Modred says we've had a jump malfunction. I agree. I think we're hung up in the between, but what I have on instruments looks like the ship is intact. Do you understand me, lady Dela?"

"Get us out!" she screamed.

"I'm trying, lady. First I have to know where we are."

And to anyone who was thinking, that answered it, because even I knew enough to know we weren't anywhere at all that our instruments were ever going to make sense of.

Com was open. There were voices in from all over, like tiny wailings. I could make out either Lynette or Vivien, and Percivale and Lancelot. And Griffin, giving orders.

"I can't," Gawain was saying. It was to his credit that he didn't blank, nor did Modred; but this was not an emotional crisis, this was business, and we were in dire trouble with things to do—if we could do them under these conditions.

I shivered, thinking that I had to navigate the corridors and somehow get to lady Dela. I clung to something solid on the bridge, trying to remember what the hallways looked like down to the last doorway, the last bolt in the walls, because if I forgot, I could get very, very lost.

"We may have been here a while," Modred's voice came to me out of the surges of color that filled my vision, and I made him out, black and slim, in front of the pool of lights. "Our senses are adjusting to interpret by new rules. If we're very careful, we should be able to keep our balance and find our way about."

"How long?" I asked. "How long can we have been here?"

"We play games with time and space both," Gawain's near-far voice returned, loud and soft by turns. "Jump . . . does that. Only we haven't come out of it. We're somewhere in subspace. And in the between, *haven't* is as good a prediction as we can make."

"Time," said Modred, "is the motion of matter; and relatively speaking, we're in a great deal of trouble. We don't know how long. It means nothing."

I grasped that. Not that I understood jump, but I knew that when ships crossed lightyears of distance by blinking here and there through jump, there had to be some kind of state in between, and that was why we took the drugs, not to have to remember that. But of course we were remembering it now: we were sitting in it, or moving through it, and whether time was stretched and we were living all this in seconds or whether we were really what Modred and Gawain

said—hung—my mind balked from such paradoxes. *They*
juggled such things, Gawain and Modred and Percy and
Lynn, but I had no desire to.

All at once Lynette came wading through the red and
black toward us, stained with the glow that was everywhere,
and walking steadily. It was a marvelous feat, that she had
gotten from the lower decks up here, and gotten to her post,
but there she was, and she pushed me out of the way and sat
down in the phantom of a chair, reached into the pool of
lights and started trying to make sense of things.

"Percy's coming," she said. And he was. I could see him
too, like a ghost striding across the distances which behaved
themselves better than they had been doing a moment ago.
Everyone was getting to their posts, and I knew mine. I stood
up and reached out my hands so that I wouldn't crack my
skull and I walked, having less trouble about it than I feared.
Spatial relationships were still giving me trouble, so that
things looked flat one moment and far away the next, but I
kept my arms out for balance and touched the sides of the
corridors when I could, shutting my eyes whenever the chaos
got too bad.

It meant going far back through the ship, and the corridor
writhed like a transparent snake with a row of lights down its
spine. At times I shut my eyes and felt my way, but the
nerves in my hands kept going numb from time to time and
the walls I couldn't see felt sticking-cold and burning hot if I
let them.

But they were only feelings, lies my senses tried to tell me,
and once and long ago I had lived in that white place where
only the tapes are real—where I got so good at seeing that I
could make pictures crawl across the walls of my cell just
as if the tapes were really running. Reality ... that doubtful
commodity that I had learned to play games with a long time
ago, because my own reality was dubious: I knew how to
make up what I liked; and I had flown and flashed from
world to world with my lady Dela; and I had sat in country
meadows under blue skies at Brahmani Dali and talked to
simpler-trained servants who thought the blue was all there
was, and who patted the ground and said that *that* was
real—but I knew it wasn't. Their up and down was all relative, and their sitting still was really moving, because their
world was moving and their sun was moving and the whole

relational space of stars was spinning out in the whirlpool eddy of *this* galaxy in the scattering of all galaxies in the flinging-forth that was time.

But their time, these servants' time, was the slow ticking away of decay in their cells, and in the motion of a clock toward the date that they would be put down, and their reality would end.

They would have gone crazy here, walking down a heaving belly of a snake in that place which somehow bucked the flinging-outward that made all they knew; and *I* did not break down, being sensible, and having an idea from the beginning that it was all like the tapes back in the labs, that told our senses what to feel and do and pay attention to. There was no sense being emotional over it: new tapes, new information.

So I kept telling myself, but my nerves still would not obey the new rules and my brain kept trying to tell me I was falling and my stomach wanted to tell me I was upside down.

I sent strong orders to my eyes. The wall straightened itself marvelously well when I really bore down on it, but shadow was really shadow, like holes into nothing. Like snippets cut out of the universe. I saw space crawling there, with hints of chaos.

Left turn. I felt for a doorswitch, wondering if anything was going to work with the ship where it was, but com had worked; and the instruments back in controls were still working, even if they picked up nothing sensible. And the door did open.

I kept going, down a corridor which seemed nightmarishly lengthened. The door at my right was open, and these were my lady's compartments. I held out my hands and walked along quite rapidly now, felt my way through the misshapen door.

Someone was sobbing, a throaty, hoarse sound that moaned through the walls: that guided me. I tripped over something that went away like chimes, over and over again, caught myself on something else I could not recognize and tried to get my bearings. There were points of light, shimmers of metal—the artificial flame lamps and the old weapons that Dela loved. That puddle of color up/down? was one of the banners, a lion in gold and red and blue. And beyond that puddle was a doorway I knew. I went to it, and through the corridor inside, to the open door of her bedroom . . . a lake of blue, a great midnight blue bed, and a cluster of shapes amid it.

My companions . . . they had reached her. Lance sat there holding my lady in his arms, and Viv huddled next to him.

"Who is it?" my lady wailed.

I came and joined myself to the others, and we held and comforted her. "It's all right," Lance kept saying. "It's all right." And I: "You know our faces. *Look* at us and everything will be what you tell it to be. It's Elaine. Elaine. Tell your eyes what they should see, and make them believe it."

"Elaine." Her hands found my face, felt for it, as if to be sure. "Go. Go help Griffin. Where is Griffin?"

"He's well," I said. "I heard him giving Wayne orders."

"Go," she pleaded, so abjectly I knew she was upsetting herself. I gathered myself up and steadied my own nerves, felt Lance's hand clinging to mine. I pulled loose of it, reached out my own toward the doorway and found it—better, much better now that I had walked this way once. I forced the room into shape and got to the corridor, felt my way along it past the library doors on the left and toward Griffin's door at the end. I got it open and a voice bellowed out at me, echoing round and round in my head.

Griffin was sick, blind sick and raving. I found the bed, found him, and stripped sheets to do what I could to comfort him. He lay on the mattress and writhed, and when I tried to make him be still he fetched me a blow that flung me rolling. It was some few moments before I could clear the haze from my eyes again, with the floor going in and out of touch with my hands, but I made it behave itself, felt the carpet, made myself see the texture of it. When I could sit up and rub the starbursts from my eyes, Griffin was sitting up and complaining; and demanding Gawain get us out of this place.

"Can't, sir," I said, hanging on the back of a chair. "We're in the between and we don't know where we are."

"Get away from me," he said. I couldn't, because my lady had told me to stay, but I pulled myself around to the front of the chair and sat down there with my knees tucked up in my arms, listening to Griffin swear and watching him stumble about the room knocking into furniture.

Eventually he discovered what we had discovered already, that he could control his stomach, and see things, and he finally seemed to get his bearings. He stood there the longest time, holding onto the dressing counter and looking at me with an expression on his face that clearly said he had not known I was there. He straightened back, stood up, felt with spidery moves of his hands toward the wall close by him. Ashamed. That was clear. And that surprised me despite everything else, because it was the first time Griffin had ever looked at me, really seemed to notice whether I existed. He turned away, groped after the bed and threw the remnant of the bedclothes over the side. Then he sat down and leaned his head into his hands, in brittle control of things. I think it took Griffin longest of all of us because he was used to having his own way, and when the whole world stopped being what suited him, it really frightened him. But our lady Dela, who lived in fantasies, she was mobile enough to attack the corridors, and showed up unexpectedly, using Lance for her help, and with Vivien trailing anxiously after.

"Worthless," lady Dela snapped at me, finding me still perched on a chair and her precious Griffin evidently neglected, sitting on the bed. I started to warn my lady when she swept down on Griffin, but at least he refrained from hitting her. He cursed and shook her hand off . . . her precious Griffin, I thought, who had never once asked about Dela.

"Out," Dela ordered me, so I got up and left her to her ministries and her lover, finding the floor a great deal plainer than it had been and the walls at least solid. I walked out, and she cursed Lance and Viv too, telling them they ought to be about their proper business, so I waited for them outside, and caught Lance's hand and held onto it for comfort when they came outside the door. What we were supposed to be doing, what our business was now, I had no least idea. Lance looked vastly shaken. Vivien looked worse than that, her eyes like one vast bruise, her hair disheveled, her fingers locked like claws on Lance's other arm, as if she were afraid he would dissolve at any moment. I reckoned that Vivien, who was so very good at books and figures, really had the least concept of all what had happened to the *Maid* and to her; she was narrow, was Viv, and so long as her accounts balanced, that was enough. Now they did not.

"I think maybe we should get Viv to bed," I said, and Lance pried her fingers loose and took her hand. We put our arms about her and guided her between us, all the long con-

fusing way back to the lift; and that was the worst, that little
loss of vertical stability after all the rest had been ripped
away from us. Viv simply moaned, too dignified to scream,
and leaned on us. We got her out again at the bottom and
back to the crew quarters. She was better when we had put
her into bed, not troubling to undress her. I tucked the sheet
up over her and Lance patted her forehead and got her a
drink, holding her head with great tenderness despite all his
own distress. It seemed strange how Lance and I managed
better than Dela and Griffin and even Vivien, who until now
had managed our lives and told us what to do. But we didn't
have to cope with the whys and the what-nows, just do little
things like walk the halls and keep ourselves on our feet. The
ones I least envied in this calamity were the *Maid*'s crew,
who were up in controls trying to figure where we were and
even when—with no reference points.

. . . but Arthur with a hundred spears
Rode far, till o'er the illimitable reed,
And many a glancing plash and sallowy isle,
The wide-wing'd sunset of the misty marsh
Glared on a huge machicolated tower. . . .

IV

Hour by hour, if that was really a word we could use any
longer, the world grew clearer, and Vivien confessed she
would live. Then came peevish orders from my lady, who
complained she was deserted by the whole staff: she wanted
Lance—which meant Griffin was better, I reckoned, since she
sounded more angry than hysterical.

Lance went off in his pained despair, called up there to be
near Griffin, which he hated, and with Dela, which was all he
ever wanted. That left us with Vivien in the crew quarters
then, in disfavor, I suspected. Vivien had drifted into quiet,
exhausted, and we had given her a little sedative we had had
ready for jump, belatedly, but it let Viv rest, not quite out,
not really tracking on much either. And in a ship the walls of
which were none too stable yet in my senses . . . the lonely
quiet seemed to put me all too far from everyone else. I was
also conscious suddenly that my stomach was terribly empty.
If time had gone as wrong as we thought it might have, then
it might have been a long while that we had not wanted food
or water, but now it hit me all of a sudden, so that I found
my limbs shaking, as if all the demands of some long depri-
vation were coming due.

And sure enough about the same time came Lynette's
voice ordering one of us to get food up to the bridge as

quickly as we could, claiming they felt faint. I was not sure that my lady Dela and particularly Griffin or Viv wanted to see food yet, but I staggered down to the lift and out on the lowermost level to the galley, and tried to put food for all of us together, out of the shambles our wild careering into jump had made of the place.

Then Vivien showed up in the doorway, a little frayed about the edges, it was true, muzzy with the drug, but moving along without touching the walls. She said nothing. Her face was set and determined with more fortitude than I had reckoned existed in Viv, and she had put most of the strands of her hair back into place so that she looked more herself. She was hungry, that was what: discomfort had gotten her moving again the same way it had sent her to bed, and without a by-your-leave she started into one of the trays. So had I, truth to tell. I had been stealing a bite and a drink while I was making the rest, because I wanted to stay on my feet to do it.

"Do they know anything yet?" she asked.

"No," I said. I refrained from adding that they weren't going to, not to pull the props out from under Viv a second time. The intercom came on: "My lady Dela wants a breakfast sent up," Lynette advised me, from the bridge, and I frowned: it was a lunch I had just put together. "If she wants it quick," I said back, "she can have a lunch that's ready. She'd have to wait ten minutes for the breakfast."

A delay. "She wants it now," Lynette relayed back. "Anything."

"It's coming." I stacked up the trays in a carrier, along with the coffee, looked up at the sound of a step in the corridor. Lance showed up and leaned there in the doorway, a shadow of himself. "Tray for you too," I said. "Here."

"She's sent for breakfast."

"I got the call. She takes what she can. Here." I put a hot roll into his hand and he ate that while I finished stacking the other carrier for the crew. I gave Dela and Griffin's carrier to Lance.

"I'll go," Vivien said, swallowing down her milk. She dried her hands, wiped possible wrinkles from her clothing. "I'll go with you."

Lance nodded, the carrier in one hand. He left, and Vivien went with her arm locked in his . . . up where Dela was. I might have gone. I might be where there was Dela to make sense of things. But I remembered the other carrier and Lynette, the whole crew up there, and then I realized what Vivien had done, leaving the work all to me.

I picked it up, grabbed another roll for myself and carried the box to the lift, rode it up, swallowing a mouthful of the roll and trying to keep my stomach down as well.

They were anxious for the food when I arrived, shadow-eyed and miserable. Percivale came and took the carrier from me and passed it round, looked puzzled at me when there were not enough. "I had a roll down below," I said, settling on a counter edge, still chewing the last of it and knowing it must sound as if I had fed myself first of all. "While it was in the oven."

They said nothing, but peeled back the covers and drank out of cups that shook in their hands . . . working harder than the rest of us and using up their reserves far faster, I thought, wishing I could have hurried it. As for me, I could go now to my lady, find what comfort there was now in her—but that was none, I thought. The screens all looked full of the same bad news. "Where are we?" I asked, after lingering there a moment, after they had at least had a chance to get a few swallows of the food down. "What's happening? Can you tell anything?" I thought—if there was any hope, I would like to take it to Dela. But they would have done that: they would have called her at once, if there were.

"We're nowhere," Lynette said sourly.

"But moving," said Modred.

The idea made me queasy. "Where?"

Modred waved a hand at the screen nearest Percy. It showed nothing I could read, but there were a lot of numbers ticking along on it.

"We've tried the engines," said Gawain. "We're moving, but we don't get anything. You understand? We've tried to affect our movement, but what works in realspace won't work here at all, wherever here is. We've tried the jump field and it won't generate. We don't know whether there's something the matter with the vanes or whether we just can't generate a field while we're in this space. Nothing works. We're without motive power. No one's ever been here before. No one knows the rules. Jumpships only skim this place. We're *in* it."

I nodded, sick at my stomach, having gotten the bad news I had bargained for.

"But there's something out there," Percivale said. "That—" He indicated the same screen Modred had. "That's a reading coming in, relative motion; and it's getting stronger."

I thought of black holes and other disquieting things, all impossible considering the fact that we were still alive and functioning, and kept arguing with myself that we had been safe where nothing like this should have happened, in the trafficked vicinity of a very normal star—which might or might not be normal now, the nasty thought kept recurring. And what about all the rest of the traffic which had been out there with us when we went popping unexpectedly into jump, presumably with some kind of field involved, which could tear ships apart and disrupt all kinds of material existence. Like planets. Like stars. If it were big enough.

"How—fast—are we moving?" I asked.

"Can't get any meaningful referents. None. Something's there, in relation to which we're moving, but the numbers jump crazily. The size of it, whether the thing we're picking up is even solid in any sense . . . or just some ghost . . . we don't know. We get readings that hold up a while and then they fall apart."

"Are we—falling into something?"

"Can't tell," said Modred, with the same calm he would have used ordering another cup of coffee.

I sat there a long time, letting the fright and the food settle. By now to my eyes the ship interior had taken on normal aspects, and my companions looked like themselves again. I reckoned that the same sort of thing must be happening with all of us, that about the time our bodies began to trouble us for normal things like food, our sensory perceptions were beginning to arrange themselves into some kind of order too.

We wouldn't starve, I thought, not—quickly. The lockers down there had the finest food, everything for every whim of my lady. The best wines and delicacies imported from faraway worlds. An enormous amount of it. We wouldn't run out of air. The interior systems were getting along just fine and nothing had shut down, or we would have had alarms sounding by now. Bad air or starving would be easiest, at least for us, who would simply blank and die.

I was terrified of the thing rushing up at us, or that we were rushing down into, or drifting slowly, whatever it was that those figures meant . . . because we had just had a bad taste of being where we were not designed to be, and another fall of any length did not sit well with my stomach.

But we could take a long time to hit and it seemed there was nothing to be done about the situation. I stood up, brushed my suit out of wrinkles. "I'm going to see my lady," I said. "Is there anything I can tell her?"

"Tell her," Gawain said, "we're trying to keep the ship intact."

I stared at him half a beat, chilled cold, then left the bridge and walked back out through the corridors which now looked like corridors . . . back to my lady's compartments.

Griffin was there when I arrived. They had gotten him up and mobile at least, into the blue bedroom, to sit at a small table and pick at the food. My lady sat across from him. I could see them through the open door. And Viv and Lance waited outside the bedroom doors, Vivien sitting on a small straight chair which had ridden through the calamity in its transit bolts. Lance was picking up bits of something which had shattered on the carpet, and some of the tapestries were crooked in their hangings.

I sat down too, in a chair which offered some comfort to my shivery limbs. Lance finished his cleaning up and took the pieces out, came back and paced the floor. I did not. I sat rigidly still, my fingers clenched on the upholstery. I was thinking about falling into some worse hole in space than we had already met, feeling that imagined motion of those figures on the bridge screen as if it were a hurtling rush.

"Where are we?" Vivien asked, my former question. Her voice was hushed and hoarse.

"In strange space," I said. And then, because it had to be said: "The crew doesn't really expect we're going to get out of it."

It was strange who came apart and who did not. Lance, who was always so vain and so worried about his appearance and his favor with my lady—he just stood there. But Vivien sat and shivered and finally blanked on us, which was the best state for her, considering her upset, and we did not move to rouse her.

"I think," Lance said, looking on her sitting frozen in her chair, "that Vivien planned to live a long, long time."

Of course that was true. Poor Vivien, I thought. All her plans. All her work. She stayed blanked, and kept at it, and finally Lance went over to her and patted her shoulder, so that she came out of it. But she slipped back again at once.

"It's a ship," Percivale's voice broke over the intercom uninvited. "It's another ship we're headed for."

That brought my lady and Griffin out of their bedroom refuge, all in a rush of moved chairs. "Signal it!" my lady ordered, looking up at the sitting room speaker panel as if it could show her something. "Contact it!"

Evidently they were doing something on the bridge, because there was silence after, and the lot of us stood there—all of us on our feet in the sitting room but Viv. Lance was shaking her shoulder and trying to get through her blankness to tell her there was some hope.

"We're not sure about the range," Modred reported finally. "We'll keep trying as we get nearer."

Griffin and lady Dela settled on a couch there near us, and we turned from Vivien to try to make them comfortable. Lady Dela looked very pale and drawn, which with her flaxen hair was pale indeed, like one of the ladies in the fantasies she loved; and Griffin too looked very shaken. "Get wine," I said, and Lance did that. We even poured a little for ourselves, Lance and I, out of their way, and got some down Vivien, holding the glass in her hand for her.

"We don't seem to be moving rapidly in relation to it," came one of Modred's calm reports, in the aching long time that passed.

"We are in Hell," my lady said after yet another long time, speaking in a hoarse, distant voice. This frightened me on the instant, because I had heard about Hell in the books, and it meant somewhere after dying. "It's all something we're dreaming while we fall, that's what it is."

I thought about it: it flatly terrified me.

"A jump accident," Griffin said. "We are *somewhere*. It's not the between. Our instruments are off, that's all. We should fix on some star and go to it. We can't have lost ourselves that far."

There were no stars in the instruments I had seen on the bridge. I swallowed, recalling that, not daring to say it.

"We have *died*," my lady said primly, calmly, evidently having made up her mind to that effect, and perhaps after the shock and the wine she was numb. "We're all dead from the moment of the accident. Brains perhaps function wildly when one dies . . . like a long dream, that takes in everything in a lifetime and stretches a few seconds into forever . . . Or this is Hell and we're in it."

I shivered where I sat. There were a lot of things that tapes had not told me, and one of them was how to cope with thoughts like that. My lady was terrifying in her fantasies.

"We're alive," Lance said, unasked. "And we're more comfortable than we were."

"Who asked you?" Dela snapped, and Lance bowed his head. We don't talk uninvited, not in company, and Griffin was company. Griffin seemed to be intensely bothered, and got up and paced the floor.

It did not help. It did not hasten the time, which crept past at a deadly slow pace, and finally Griffin spun about and strode out the door.

"Griffin?" my lady Dela quavered.

I stood up; Dela had; and Lance. "He mustn't give orders," I said, thinking at least where I would be going if I were Griffin, and we heard the door to the outside corridor open, not that to his own rooms. "Lady Dela, he's going to the bridge. He mustn't give them orders."

My lady stared at me and I think if she had been close enough she might have hit me. But then her face grew afraid. "They wouldn't pay any attention to him. They wouldn't."

"No, lady Dela, but he's strong and quick and I'm not sure they could stop him."

Dela stirred herself then and made some haste. Lance and I seized up Viv and drew her along in Dela's wake, out into the corridors and down them to the bridge. It was all, all too late if Griffin had had something definite in mind; but it was still peaceful when we arrived, Griffin standing there in the center of the bridge and the crew with their backs to him and working at their posts. Griffin was ominous looking where he was, in the center of things, hands on hips. None of the crew was particularly big . . . only Lance was that, the two of them like mirrors, dark and gold, the lady's taste running remarkably similar in this instance. And Lance made a casual move that took himself between Griffin and Gawain and Lynn at main controls, just standing there, in case.

"Well?" Dela asked.

"We don't have contact," Percivale said, beside Modred. "We keep sending, but the object doesn't respond. We were asked about range: we don't know that either. Everything has failed."

"Where *is* this thing we're talking about?" Dela asked, and Modred reached and punched a button. It came up on the big screen, a kind of a cloud on the scope, all gridded and false, just patches of something solid the computer was trying to show us.

"I think we're getting vid," Percivale said, and that image went off, replaced with another, in all the flare of strange colors and shapes that drifted where there ought to be stars, in between blackness measled with red spots like dapples that might be stars or just the cameras trying to pick up something that made no sense. And against that backdrop was something that might be a misshapen world in silhouette, or a big rock irregularly shaped, or something far vaster than we wanted to think, no knowing. It was flattened at its poles and it bristled with strange shapes in prickly complexity.

"We've been getting nearer steadily," Modred said. "It could be our size or star-sized. We don't know."

"You've got the scan on it," Griffin snapped at him. "You've got that readout for timing."

"Time is a questionable constant here," Modred said without turning about, keeping at his work. "I refrained from making unjustified assumptions. This is new input on the main screen. I am getting a size estimate.—Take impact precautions. Now."

Near . . . we were coming at it. It was getting closer and closer on the screen. My lady caught at Griffin, evidently having given up her theory of being dead. "Use the engines," Griffin yelled at Gawain and Lynn, furious. "If we're coming up against some mass they may react off that . . . use the engines!"

"We are," Gawain said calmly.

We grabbed at both Dela and Griffin, Lance and I, and pulled them to the cushioned corner and got the bar down and the straps round them, then dragged Vivien, who was paralyzed and nearly blanked, with us to the remaining pad.

The crew was putting the safety bars in place too, all very cool. That we couldn't feel the engines . . . no feel to them at all . . . when normally they should have been kicking us hard in some direction. . . .

Screens broke up. We were just too close to it. It had filled all our forward view and the last detail we got was huge. Something interfered with the pickup. I wrapped the restraints about myself while Lance did his, and all the while expected the impact, to be flung like some toy across a breached compartment on a puff of crystalizing air. . . . I didn't know what was out there, but the most horrible fate of all seemed to me to be blown out of here, to be set adrift naked in *that*, whatever that stuff was out there. This little ship that held our lives also held whatever sanity we had been able to trick our eyes into seeing, and what was out there—I wondered how long it took to die in that stuff. Or whether one ever did.

The last buckle jammed. I refitted it, in sudden tape-taught calm. I was with the ship and my lady. I had my referents. My back was to the wall and my most favorite comrades were with me. I didn't want to end, but there was comfort in company—far better, I conned myself, than what waited for us by our natures, to be taken separately by the law and coldly done away. This was like born-men, this was—

"Repulse is working," Gawain said, about the instant my stomach felt the slam of the engines. "Stop rotation."

Don't! I thought irrationally, because I trusted nothing to start working again once it had been shut down in this mad place, and if rotation stopped working the way it did when we would go into a dock at station, we would end up null G in this stuff, subject to its laws. We were not, for mercy's sake, coming in at a safe dock with crews waiting to assist, and there was no place to put the *Maid*'s delicate nose-probe, all exposed out there.

G started going away. We were locking into station-docking position, the crew going through their motions with heart-breaking calm, doing all the right things in this terrible place; and the poor unsecured *Maid* was going to be chaos in her station-topside decks.

A touch came at my fingers. It was Lancelot's hand seeking mine. I closed on it, and reached beside me for Vivien's, which was very cold.

She had, Lance had said it, planned to live, and everything was wrong for her. No hope for Vivien, whose accounts and knowledge were useless now. I understood suddenly, that Vivien's function was simply gone for her; and she had already begun to die, in a way as terrible as being dumped out in the chaos-stuff.

"The lady will need you," I hissed at Viv, gripping her nerveless hand till I ground the bones together. "She needs us all."

That might have helped. There was a little jerk from Viv's hand, a little resistance; and I winced, for Lance closed down hard on mine. My lady and Griffin screamed—we hit, ground with a sound like someone was shredding the *Maid*'s metal body, and our soft bodies hit the restraints as the ship's mass stopped a little before that of our poor flesh. I blanked half an instant, came out of it realizing pain, and that somehow we had not been going as fast as I feared a ship might in this place (which estimate ranged past C and posed interesting physics for collision) or what we had hit was going the same general direction as we were, at an angle. Mass, I thought, if that had any meaning in this place/time . . . a monstrous mass, to have pulled us into it, if that was what it had done. Our motion had not stopped in collision. The noise had not. We grated, hit, hung, grated, a shock that seemed to tear my heart and stomach loose.

"We're up against it," Modred's cool voice came to me. "We'd better grapple or we'll go on with this instability."

Instability. A groaning and scraping, and a horrifying series of jolts, as if we were being dragged across something. The *Maid* shifted again, her dragging force of engines like a hand pushing us.

Clang and thump. I heard the grapples lock and felt the whole ship steady, a slow suspicion of stable G that crawled through the clothes I wore and settled my hair down and caressed my abused joints and stomach and said that there was indeed up and down again. It was a kilo or so light, but we had G. Whatever we were fixed to had spin and we had gotten our right orientation to *it*.

The crew was still exchanging quiet information, doing a shutdown, no cheers, no exuberance in their manner. That huge main screen cleared again, to show us ruby-spotted blackness and our own battered nose with the grapples locked

onto something. Strong floods were playing from our hull
onto the surface we faced, a green, pitted surface which was
flaring with colors into the violets and dotted with little insta-
bilities like black stars. It made me sick to look at it; but it
was indeed our nose probe, badly abraded and with stuff
coming out of it like trailing cable or black snakes, and there
was our grapple locked into something that looked like metal
wreckage. The lights swung further and it was wreckage, all
right, some other ship all dark and scarred and crumpled.
The lights and camera kept traveling and there was still another ship, of some delicate kind I had never imagined. It
was dark too, like spiderweb in silhouette, twisted wreckage
at its heart with its filament guts hanging out into the red
measled void.

My lady Dela swore and wept, a throaty, loud sound in the
stillness about us now. She freed herself of the restraints and
crossed the deck to Gawain and Lynn, and Griffin came at
her heels. I loosed myself, and Lance did, while Dela leaned
there on the back of Gawain's chair, looking up at the screen
in terror. Griffin set his big hands on her shoulders. "Keep
trying," Griffin asked of the crew, who kept the beam and the
cameras moving, turning up more sights as desolate. Aft,
through the silhouette of the *Maid*'s raking vanes, there was
far perspective, chaos-stuff with violet tints into the red.
More wreckage then. The cameras stopped. "There," Modred
said. "There."

It was a curve, lit in the queasy flarings, a vast sweep, a
symmetry in the wreckage, as if the thing we were fixed to
were some vast ring. Ship bodies were gathered to it like parasites, like fungus growth, with red and black beyond, and the
wrecks themselves all spotted with holes as if they were eaten
up with acid light . . . illusion of the chaos-stuff, or something showing through their metal wounds, like glowing
blood.

"Whatever we've hit," Percy said quietly, "a lot have gone
before us. It's some large mass, maybe a station, maybe a
huge ship—once. Old . . . old. Others might fall through the
pile into us the same way we've hit them."

"Then get us out of here," my lady said. "Get us out!"

Gawain and Lynette stirred in their seats. Wayne powered
his about to look up at her. "My lady Dela, it's not possible."
He spoke with the stillest patience. "We can wallow about the

surface, batter ourselves into junk against it. If we loose those grapples we'll do that."

I thought she would hit him. She lifted her hand. It fell. "Well, what are you going to do?"

Gawain had no answer. Griffin set his hands on my lady's arms, just stood there. I looked at Lance and he was white; I looked at Vivien and she plainly blanked, standing vacant-eyed in her restraints. I undid them, patted her face hard until I got a flicker in her eyes, put my arms about her and held her. She wrapped her arms about me and held on.

"The hull is sound," Modred said. "Our only breach is *G*-34. I've sealed that compartment."

"Get us out of here," Dela said. "Fix what's wrong with us and get us out of here, you hear that? You find out how to move in this stuff and get us away."

The crew slowly stopped their operations, confronted with an impossibility. I held to Viv, and Lance just stood there, his hand clenched on one of the safety holds. I felt a profound cold, as if it were our shared fault, this disaster. We had failed and the *Maid* was damaged—more than damaged. All the crew's skill, that had stopped our falling, that had docked us here neatly as if it was Brahmani Station . . . in this terrible, terrible place. . . .

"We're fixed here," Lynette said. "There's no way. There's no repair that can make the engines work against this. The *Maid* won't move again. Can't."

There was stark silence, from us, from Dela, no sound at all over the ship but the fans and the necessary machinery.

"How long will we survive?" Griffin asked. He kept his steadying hold on my lady. His handsome face was less arrogant than I had ever seen it; and he came up with the only sensible question. "What's a reasonable estimate?"

"No immediate difficulty," Gawain said. He unfastened his restraints and stood up, jerking his head so that his long hair fell behind his shoulders. "Modred?"

"The ship is virtually intact," Modred said. "We're not faced with shutdown. The lifesupport and recycling will go on operating. Our food is sufficient for several years. And for the percentage of inefficiency in the recycling, there are emergency supplies, frozen cultures, hydroponics. It should be indefinite."

"You're talking about living here," Dela said in a faint voice.

"Yes, my lady."

"In *this*?"

Modred turned back to his boards, without answer.

Dela stood there a moment, slowly brought her hands up in front of her lips. "Well," she said in a tremulous voice, with a sudden pivot and look at Griffin, at all of us. "Well, so we do what we can, don't we?" She looked at the crew. "Who knows anything about the hydroponics?"

"There's a training tape," Percy said, "in library. It's a complicated operation. When the ship is secured—"

"I can do that." Vivien stirred at my side, muscles tensing. "Lady Dela, I'll do that."

Dela looked at her, waved her hand. "See to it." Viv shivered, with what joy Dela surely had no concept. Sniffed and straightened her back. Dela paced the deck, distracted, with that look in her eyes—panic. It was surely panic. She laughed a faint and brittle laugh and came back and laced her fingers into Griffin's hand. "So we make the best of it," she said, looking up at him. "You and I."

He stood looking at the screens and the horror outside, while my lady Dela put her arms about him. Maybe she was building her fantasies back again, but it was a different look I saw on Griffin's face, which was not resigned, which was set in a kind of desperation. My jaw still ached where he had hit me in his panic, and I was afraid of this man as I would have been afraid of one of my own kind who had had such a lapse —for which one of *us* might have been put down. But born-men were entitled to stupidities, and to be forgiven for them.

What was outside our hull didn't forgive. We were snugged by some attraction up against a huge mass. Even if the big generation vanes were to work in this vicinity as the repulse had—from what little I knew of jump, I knew we dared not try, not unless we wanted to string our components and bits of that mass into some kind of fluxing soup . . . half to stay here and half to fly off elsewhere. That mass was going to serve to keep us here, one way or the other.

A wandering instability, a knot in time and space, a ripple in the between that came wandering through our safe solar system and sucked us up. And with who knew what other

ships? I almost opened my mouth on that sudden thought—
that perhaps we should try to see if we had company in this
disaster, if others had been sucked through too; material
things seemed to work here, and maybe the com would. And
then I thought of some big passenger carrier, short of food
and water in relation to its number of passengers, and what
that might mean for *us*, if they did make contact.

No. Old—Percy had said it. Perhaps—the thought went
shivering through my flesh while I stared at the screens—others had faced similar moments, had lived out their lives until
they decayed, the light eating through them. From what we
had seen of the mass, from the insane way in which the ships
were fused, one upon the other, they must all be very old, if
age meant anything at all here, and that was not the quick
eating away of matter by the chaos-stuff.

"Go," my lady said suddenly, waving her hands at us. "See
what's damaged. Start putting things in order. See to it. Are
you going to stand like you've lost your wits?"

I looked desperately at Lance and Vivien, turned and went,
a last backward look at the screens, and then I hurried out to
check the halls and the compartments. My lady now talked as
if she had given up her premise that we were dead, and I
took some comfort in that while I walked the corridors back
to her compartment—only mild damage there. The wine
bottle had been mostly empty, the dew had been so generally
distributed in null-G that there remained no visible trace of it
except on the tabletops and the steel doors. The rest had
soaked into the carpet and covered the woodwork, beyond
helping. And the glasses were unbreakable, lying where returning G had dropped them. I wiped surfaces, straightened
the bed, gathered up fallen towels in the bath. At least there
had been no furniture out of its braces. Not so bad. I walked
outside, confronted suddenly with the chill corridors, the light
G that made my stomach queasy. It came back to me again
what my lady had said about eternity being compassed in dying, about the brain spilling all it contained in random
firings—but then, if that were so, then we should not be sharing the dream, unless all that I had touched, the ship, the
lady, Lance, everyone—was illusion, and I had never seen or
touched at all.

Perhaps I had built it all out of the chaos-stuff as I had
built my hand when I willed to see it. Perhaps I had just gone

too far in my building, and what the lady said about dying was my own brain talking to itself, trying to convince me by logic that the dream had to end and that I should be decently dead.

And I would not listen, but went on dreaming.

No, I thought, and shuddered, because there had just crept a touch of red into the shadows in the hall, the old way of looking at things coming back again, and if I could not stop it my eyes would begin to see the chaos-stuff through the walls.

They had experimented, so my lady's pilfered tapes had told me, with living human senses; and the brain could be re-educated. Eyes could learn to see rightside up or upside down. Somewhere in the waves of energy that impinged the nerves, the brain constructed its own fantasies of matter and blue skies and green grass and solidity, screening out the irrational and random.

A reality existed within us too, tides of particles that were themselves nodes in chaos, all strung together to make this reality of ours. And in this place the structure of matter gaped wide and I could see it . . . miniature tides like the tides of the moving galaxies in one rhythm with them, and us spread like a material veil between, midway of one reality and the other.

No, I thought again, and leaned against the veil/wall in my chosen viewpoint of what was, was, was . . . don't look down. One was advised not to look at such things and never to know that all of us were dreaming, dreaming even when we were sure we were alive, because what the brain always did was dream, and what difference whether it built its dreams from the energy affecting it from outside or whether it traced its own independent fancies, making its own patterns on the veil. Don't lean too hard. Don't look.

I slid down onto the corridor floor and heaved up my insides, which was my body's way of telling me it had had enough nonsense. It wanted the old dream back, insisted to have it. I lay there dry-heaving until I dismissed my ideas of dreams and eternities, because I hurt inside and wanted to die, and if I could have waked and died at once I would have gladly done it.

So a pair of slippered feet came up to me; and my lady Dela, all tearful, cursed me for useless and kicked me besides, in my sore stomach. That helped, actually, because when my lady had gone on in and shut the door, I was angry, which was better than hurting. And before I had gotten up on my own, Percy came after me, saying she had sent him. Gentle Percy cleaned the hall up and cleaned me up and carried me to the crew quarters. There, when he had gone back to his duties, I took care of myself and changed and felt better, if somewhat hollow at the gut.

So much for fighting it. I moved meekly about the reality of the *Maid*, loving her poor battered self as I did my own body, and doing all I could to get her into order again. So did we all, I think with the same reason, that if the *Maid* had been precious to us before, she was ten thousand times so now.

Then to her tower she climb'd, and took the shield,
There kept it, and so lived in fantasy.

V

It seemed a long time that we worked. The clocks said one thing and our bodies told us something else, and they were never in agreement, so that some hours flew past as if we had been daydreaming and others dragged on and on while we ached and got thirsty and hungry. I kept thinking of the way the walls had come and gone at first, and that hours were doing the same thing, or our bodies were. Whatever happened to matter, Lynn said, would happen to us; and if there were phases in this place, I reckoned, where things just went slower, then we and the clocks ought to agree, but it didn't work out that way. It was one of the small horrors that worked at our nerves and urged us that just blanking out might be better. Likewise Modred and Percy said comp went out on them: it dumped program at times, and at others behaved itself. The crew stayed on the bridge or back at the monitor station—worried, I gathered, about the power plant that kept us going—but it did go, the fans kept turning and the air kept recycling and, Gawain said when I brought them another meal, there was no real need for them to stay by controls, because what was automatic was working tolerably well and what was not automatic was not doing well at all and they couldn't fix anything, just live with it and be patient when comp dumped.

Gawain was tired. His eyes were terrible. So were Modred's, like black pits. They had been in their day cycle and had been through more than a day now. They ended by deciding perhaps they should stay up in controls after all, all of them—in case the alarms didn't function dependably. "Until we see," Modred said. So I brought up mats and pillows and blankets for the four of them and they bedded down up there.

Vivien—Viv was asleep too, busy deepstudying, locked into that tape that would make her useful again, after which time she would likely have a thousand orders to give us all. Lance was somewhere repairing damages and cleaning up, where unsecured items had smashed into walls, or unbraced chairs made wreckage of themselves. Not technical things, but such things as we could do.

Griffin called me, wanting two suppers in my lady's quarters, so I went to the galley and fixed all he asked for . . . he and my lady, who consoled each other, who had been consoling each other all afternoon of that quick/slow day. Well enough. It put no demands on us, tired as we were. I carried the trays up in a carrier and walked in with them, very quietly, into the sitting room.

I walked farther, cautiously, and I could see the big blue bed and them tangled in the middle of it, golden blond Griffin and my pale blonde lady, pink to his gold, and white, and her braids all undone in a net about them. They made love. I waited, waited longer, finally put the carrier on the mobile table and quietly as I could I eased it through the door, just to leave it where they could have it when they wanted. They never noticed my being there, or they ignored it, lost in each other, and very quietly I left and closed all the doors behind me, downcast with my own aches and pains and where we were and what hopelessness we had of doing something about it.

Sleep, I thought. I was due my rest, finally; and overdue.

And I was right outside the library.

I came in very quietly. Viv was on the couch, limp in deepsleep. She chose to do her deepstudy in the library, maybe not to bother those of us who wanted to talk in the crew quarters, but such extreme consideration was not Viv's style. It was more, I figured, out of fear of being supplanted; she wanted no rivals who could do what she could do, and she didn't want that tape in our hands.

The lights were low. I could have slapped her face and not roused her, but all the same I kept very quiet picking out the tape *I* wanted. I slipped it into my jacket and went out again, trusting Modred would cover for me when he must. Ah! I wanted the deepsleep.

I walked down the corridor to the main hall, and the lift, and so down to the crew quarters with my treasure. I undressed and bathed and in my robe set up the unit on the couch, attached the sensor leads, took the drug—thinking with melancholy that we would run out, someday—not of the tapes but of the drug that made them more intense; that when my lady thought of that . . . we would lose our supply, and she would not be long in thinking of it. It was only fair, perhaps, because *we* could sink into the tapes and the dreams so much more easily than born-men. I felt a guilt that had nothing to do with my tape-pilfering: I stole my lady's dreams. It was selfish, and bothered my psych-sets; but I rationalized it, that she had *not* forbidden it, and sank back with my tape, in it, part of it.

> Elaine the fair, Elaine the loveable,
> Elaine the lily maid of Astolat,
> High in her chamber up a tower to the east
> Guarded the sacred shield of Lancelot. . . .

It was my dream, my own, my world better than the real: my lady Dela's world; and mine. We were made, we who served, never born; we were perfect, and needed no dreams to make us more than we were created by the labs to be. We were not intended to love . . . but it was seeing born-men's sharing love that made me lonely, and made me think of my tape—

> I know not if I know what true love is,
> But, if I know, then, if I love not him,
> I know there is none other I can love. . . .

I thought of Lancelot. Probably I cried; and we don't do that generally, not like born-men, because where they would cry, we go blank. Only in the taped dreams, then we might, because there's no blanking out on them. While the tape was running, I loved, and had a soul, and believed in the bornmen's God; and when it would stop I was all hollow and frightened for a moment: that was the price, I knew, of pil-

fering tapes not meant for us. But then my other tapes, those
deep in my mind, would take over and bring me back to
sense.

> Then while Sir Lancelot leant, in half disdain
> At love, life, all things, on the window ledge,
> Close underneath his eyes, and right across
> Where these had fallen, slowly past the barge
> Whereon the lily maid of Astolat
> Lay smiling, like a star in blackest night.

I waked for real. Arms held me. I thought it was part of
the tape at first, because sensations in them were that real,
called out of the mind; but the sound had stopped, and I was
still lapped in someone's arms, and comforted. I would have
gone on into normal sleep except for that; I was conscious
enough now to fight out of it, pull the piece from my ear and
the other attachments from my temples and my body, sweeps
of a half-numb hand. My eyes cleared enough that I saw who
slept with me, that it was Lance. Like a thief he had slipped
into my dream, to share the tape while it was running . . .
the tape that he was never supposed to have. His face was
sadder than it had ever been. His eyes were closed, tears running from under his lashes. More than mine, the tape was his,
and his part was sadder than mine by far. I loved and lost
him, young and only half knowing love at all; but he, older,
having more, lost everything.

And that was always true for him.

I hurt, and maybe it was more than my psych-set that
grieved me. I was still in the haze of the tape's realities. I
swept the tiny sensors away from his brow and his heart, and
wiped the tears away for him. I kissed him, not for sex, as
my tapes are, but because it was what the real Elaine would
have done, a kind of tenderness like touching, like lying close
at night, that kind of comfort.

He waked then and embraced me purposefully, and I
shifted over, getting rid of other sensor connections, because I
was willing. I reckoned it was the best thing for him, to occupy his mind and body both after going through that dream.

But he couldn't. It was the first time he ever outright
couldn't, and it shook him. He blanked, then, which froze my
heart—because blanking out from something beyond your

limits is one thing; but blanking on your training, on your whole reason for being at all—He stayed that way a moment, and then he came out of it and rolled over and lay there with his eyes open and a terrible sorrow on his face. He shivered now and then, and I put my arms about him and pulled the sheets up about us.

"I'm sorry," he said finally without ever looking at me. I might have been anyone.

"We're all awfully tired," I said. And in my heart: O Lance, you should never have heard it, and I should never have used it here—because he had one thing that he did and that was it, and maybe he had just seen something else, yearning after that other Lancelot as I did after that other Elaine, who was absolute in love, and who was so much that I was not made to be. What was Lance's other self that *he* was not? Much, that no lab-born was ever made to be.

I wiped the last trace of tears from off his face and he did not blink. I leaned close and kissed him again.

"It does no good," he said.

"I didn't mean it that way," I said, and I didn't. I just held him and hurt for him like my own heart was breaking, because they made me that way, my psych-set was involved, and I couldn't help him. "It's a very old story," I whispered, prattling on because I knew his whole reality was upset and I had to make it make sense to him or he was in trouble. "It's the lady's fancy, that tape; and so she named us what she did when she bought us, and maybe there's a little truth in the names—because she did think about which she gave to whom, after all, and *she's* read our psych-sets—But it's a joke, Lance, it's our lady's joke, a play, a thing from very long ago and some world with nothing to do with ours. You understand that? It's not *ours*. The *Maid* is just a dream Dela takes up when she's bored. You've always known that, and it's always true. How long have you been with her?"

"Twenty years."

And me with my five, I was going to tell him what truth was. That long he had belonged to her: I had had no idea it could have been so many years, or I had never added it up and thought. Thirty six. He had been sixteen when he came to her. That long he had been fixed on her, and Dela was all his life . . . always Dela, Dela, like some guidance star his whole self was locked onto. Lover after lover she took—but Lance was always waiting when love was done.

Love—not us. Ours was a tape-fixed complex of compulsions and avoidances; pain if we turned away from our duty . . . pain, and guilt; and this horrible twisting inside, at any thought of losing what we were fixed to, and created to do.

And there was deep irony in it all, because Elaine—the real Elaine, the one realer than I—had destroyed herself trying to turn Lancelot's love to herself, when it was fixed on Guinevere: she had to try, because in the story Elaine was fixed on him and he on his lady, and that made sense within my frame of reference. I was not supposed to fix on him, but pain always went straight to my gut and made me try to stop it; and he had the most pain of anyone aboard.

That was what had happened to me when I saw him hurting like this. And because I had done this to him myself, that settled a horrible guilt on me. I lay there thinking desperately that maybe I ought to get up and go to our lady and tell her what I had done, but that was bound to bring down one of her rages, and I didn't see how it could help Lance either. The last thing he wanted, I was sure, was for Dela to find out how much he knew or that he had failed with me just now.

I had a sense of empathy: it was my training; and I put myself in Lance's place, who had always to endure these voyages in which the rest of us took pleasure, endure them and wait for Dela to tire of her new lovers and to come back to him, which she always had. But there was no coming back from this voyage; and Griffin was not getting off the ship, ever. Where that led in Lance's poor mind, I was afaid to follow. I remembered how strong he was, and I knew how desperate he was, and I knew that Griffin was both strong himself and could get desperate as this place fretted at him—and that scared me beyond wanting to think about it. One of us could never raise a hand to a born-man. An avoidance was built into us which would send us hurtling into blank long before the hand left our side.

But Griffin was dangerous. My lady had always fancied dangerous men, because there was very little in this world she could not control or predict, and she liked her games wild and enjoyed a certain feeling of risk.

It had never occurred to me before that Lance himself was dangerous. He had been there too long, too quietly, was too much one of us, bowing his head, taking even blows, accepting the worst that ever my lady's associates chose to do—

My lady chose dangerous men, and this one had been with her for twenty years, pretty as he was, and while it was always Modred strangers stepped aside for, with his dark and cold face—

Something had snapped in Lance. Maybe it would heal. Maybe like Vivien, who had gone in a single day from managing my lady's accounts to being in charge of the hydroponics which were going to keep us all alive, he would do some kind of transference and pull himself out of it. He still shivered now and again, and the look on his face stopped being pain and became a lockjawed stare at the ceiling. He blinked sometimes, so it was not a blank; and the eyes were lively, so he was thinking, in that place inside his skull to which he had gone. But his face that had always been sad was something else now, as if there had been some harsh wind blowing that he was staring into, and I was not even there.

I never was, for him. That part of the story was true.

And finally he decided he would stop thinking about whatever it was, and he got up and got dressed, while I decided I had better take the tape and hide it somewhere until I could get it to Modred, before something worse happened.

"Don't," Lance said, holding my hand with the tape in it.

"It's got to go back. I'll take it to Modred."

"He can run a copy. Can't he?" He took the tape from me. *He* put it away, in his locker. I stood watching and reckoning that he was caught in it now like I was. He would listen to it again, and it would become his as it was mine. I shared it now, like it or not.

"I wish you'd asked before coming in on me," I said.

He turned and lifted his hand to my face, touched my cheek. It was a strange gesture, for him. I could see him doing it to Dela. Then he hugged me against him like the old friend I was to him. "Don't tell her I couldn't," he asked of me.

"Of course I won't," I said. "Bed with me and sleep a while. It'll be different. You're tired, that's all."

But it wasn't different, and then I was really frightened for him; and I knew that he was scared. There began to be an even worse look on his face, that was not merely sadness, but torment, and worse still for the likes of us—anger.

He was gone the next morning, after breakfast. The whole ship was about such routine as existed in such circumstances, the crew trying to get their own equipment into order, checking out things that they knew how to do, and there had been no emergencies. Dela took to her bed again, and Griffin stayed mostly about the sitting room, what time he was not poking into things about the control room, the monitor station, and the observation dome, bedeviling the crew with worry over what he might do—grim and scowling all the while, with Dela taking pills for her nerves. A second day in this place, all too much as novel as the first, any time anyone wanted to look at the horror on the screens, and watch the acid light eating through our neighbors, or to look out on that vast dead wheel which held us all to its mass. Dela called for *that tape,* and my heart stopped; but the original, at least, was back where it belonged: Lance had seen to that, so we were safe. And soon my lady slept the deepsleep, lost in the dream.

Vivien was up and about her new business, keeping Percivale busy finding this and that for her out of storage. She had appropriated a large space topside, a private queendom into which she had brought loads of stored tanks and pipe and electronics over which Percivale sweated. So all of us were accounted for.

Except Lance, to Vivien's extreme pique.

There was no one else who had reason to think anything might be amiss. He might even be off about the lady's instructions. And Modred or others of the crew might know where he was, since he must have been on the bridge getting that duplicate tape run sometime around breakfast . . . but I was afraid to ask questions and make much of his absence.

I searched . . . quietly, between duties I had to do, between fetching Vivien this and that. And I found him finally, in almost the last place I thought to look before starting on the topside holds . . . in the gym that lay bow-ward of the galley, all by himself, drenched in sweat despite the cold in there.

I stood there in the open doorway with my heart beating hard with relief. He saw me. He said nothing, only walked on over to another of the machines and meddled with it, by which I decided he didn't want to say anything, or see any-one. He started up his exercise again as if he could force his body to do what it ought by making it stronger. Or maybe that wasn't his reason. In any event he should hardly be here when others had duties . . . but I was far from saying so.

I closed the door again, walked away to the galley, figuring that the crew might appreciate something hot to drink about now. I tried to do something useful—and all the while Lance's look kept gnawing at me, dark and sullen.

The lift worked, not far away from the galley. I heard someone come down, and went to the door, expecting maybe Percy, who was coming and going on Viv's errands. It was a man's tread.

I met Griffin.

Maybe fright showed. He looked at me and frowned, and I vacated the doorway, letting him in. "Have you seen Lancelot?" he asked, setting my heart pounding afresh. "They said he might be around the gym."

I cursed them all, the crew—who had sent Griffin down here, to get him off their necks up there, I reckoned. I even tried to think of a lie; but he was a born-man and his frown turned my bones to jelly. I nodded meekly, found a tray and some cups to occupy my sight and my hands. "I was going to make a snack, sir. Would you like?"

"You think we have enough to be making up meals off-schedule?"

I looked at him, already unnerved; and yes, I had thought of it, but the crew had needs, and the lady had given no or-ders. Griffin couldn't tell me what to do. He was a guest, not giving orders for my lady. But he had that kind of voice that made muscles flinch whether they wanted to or not. "They've been working hard up there," I said, "by your leave, sir. Would you like some?"

"No. They're not working up there. Except doing the hy-droponics setup. That." His eyes raked around the galley as if he were hunting for fault. "I'll be in the gym," he said then. "If Dela asks."

"Sir," I murmured, eyes lowered, a quick turn toward him. He left. I leaned on the counter a moment, not wanting now to do what I had set out to do as an excuse; but I was afraid to follow him.

I busied myself after a moment, not hearing him come back, made the coffee and took it up. It was what master Griffin had said, that there was not much going on about the bridge. The hateful screens stayed the same. Gawain was there alone. Modred and Lynn were out in the observation bubble—strange to have everyone on the same shift, but when I thought about it, it was not as if we would be needing the mainday/alterday rotation. Not here. Gawain called the others, and they were glad of the coffee; Percy and Viv came too, Percy in sweat-stained coveralls and Viv in a neat beige suit.

"Is Lance *fixing* something down there?" Viv asked, and then I knew who might have told Griffin, if she had found it out to tell. I frowned. "He was working over the machines," I said without a flicker. Lance had problems enough without being dragooned into Viv's merciless service. "I think he's busy."

"Huh," Vivien said, and sipped her coffee.

"What did Griffin want?" I asked. "To use the gym?"

"He asked where Lance was," Percy said.

"I'd been looking for him," I said.

"Griffin?"

"Lance."

"Could have asked," Modred said.

I fretted, sipped my own coffee. "I'd think he'd have come back by now."

"Griffin? He's been everywhere this morning. Insisted to have us explain controls to him."

"He's handled insystem craft," Gawain said tartly. "He says. Elaine—drop a word to my lady. The *Maid* isn't in a position we can afford difficulties. You understand."

"I'll try," I said, looking at my coffee instead of at the screens, with their terrible red images. "I'll do it when she wakes up."

It made me cold, that worry of Gawain's, and this restlessness of Griffin's. Griffin, who was down in the gym; with Lance—in his frame of mind.—Why aren't you working? I could hear Griffin asking Lance, meddling-wise. What are you doing down here? And I could see Lance with that sullenness in his expression, that hurt that was there, exploding—

I put my cup empty onto the tray. Gawain did. The others

lingered drinking theirs, so I had no excuse to go. "I think I may have left a switch on in the galley," I said.

"Comp can check it," Percy said.

I abandoned excuses and left the bridge, forgetting the tray, hurried to the lift and rode it back down to the lower-most level, walked quickly down the dim corridor forward.

The gym door was open. I walked into that echoing place with its exercise machines and its padded walls, hearing grunts and crashes, and my heart stopped in me, seeing the two of them, Lance and Griffin, locked in fighting. And then I saw them more clearly, that they were wrestling, stripped down. They grappled and shifted for advantage. It was sport, a game

—and not. They struggled, bled where fingers gripped, strained and heaved strength against strength. Muscles shivered and shifted blinding quick. They broke, panting, eye to eye, shifted and charged again, seeking new advantage, making the echoes ring. Both were sleek with sweat, both matched height for height and reach for reach, in weight and width of shoul-der and length of arm and leg. Dark head beside bright, olive skin next golden, they turned and moved and strained, locked in a grip that neither one would give up, and I ached watch-ing it, turned half away, for it seemed that bones and joints must crack . . . looked again, and they seemed blind to all else, still locked, glassy-eyed, each trying to make the other yield. A born-man, in contest with one of us. And that one of us could fight a born-man, even in sport—

I knew why Lance wrestled, and what he fought, and I was cold inside.

Lance, O Lance, it's not a game.

Not for either of them.

"Griffin," I cried. "Master Griffin!—I think you should see my lady. She's been locked away too long. Please come."

They broke. Griffin looked toward me. I ran away, but I waited in the crosspassage outside until I knew Griffin had believed my lie and was gone from there, sweaty as he was, carrying his shirt over his arm and headed for the lift.

Lance came, later. He didn't see me. I stayed to the shadows and watched him pass, walking with shoulders bowed, showered and cleaned and bearing no mark on him.

I could have bit my tongue for the lie I'd chosen, that Dela had had need of Griffin—and not of him.

At least I had stopped it. That much. What was more, it worked—at least for Dela, who got Griffin back; and for Griffin, who at least found himself welcome. No more of them that afternoon, no more intrusions on the crew, no more of Griffin's frettings.

Lance . . . helped Viv and Percy set up the lab, unnaturally patient.

That evening—evening, as we had declared the time to be—my lady decided to throw a private party—a party in Hell, she declared it, with that terrible born-man humor of hers; and we had to serve the dinner and serve as guests as well . . . to fill up the table.

Griffin fell in with this humor in reluctant grace, and dressed. It was Lance who had to attend him, Lance that Dela appointed his servant. Better me, oh, better me; but that was how it was. I dressed my lady Dela in her best, a beautiful blue gown, and did her hair, and fixed the dinner, and in betweentimes I saw to myself, and to Viv and to the crew.

The crew, for their part, was not enthusiastic. They were still on their duty fix.

"They're to enjoy themselves," was Dela's order, which I relayed. It was a kind of absolution, and that wrought a little change (at least I imagined one) in Lynn and Wayne and Percy, once they did off their plain duty clothes and changed into their best.

Vivien now preened and became her chignoned, elegant self again, fit for the halls at Brahmani Dali. It's not precisely so that Vivien couldn't love: she adored her own handsomeness. "Bring me my gown," it was; and "Careful with that," as if she were Dela. As if her clinging to me and Lance during the catastrophe embarrassed her now, so she put more feeling than usual into giving orders, and took more fussing-over than all the rest of us put together.

No fussing at all for Modred. He stayed himself, and came in black, like what he wore on duty. My lady said in seeing him that it matched his soul—but that was figurative, I took it, souls being a born-man attribute.

Griffin came; and Lance—Griffin in blue and Lance in darker blue, a color almost as grim as Modred's. We saw Griffin and Dela seated and served the wine, and hurried below to bring up the feast, Lance and I; and Percy, who was not too proud to help—smiling and chattering with easy cheerfulness. Lance put on a smile, if you didn't look at the eyes—and Percivale used the wit in that handsome skull of his and chattered blithely away while we arranged things, with a tact I think he learned on his own. Certainly his duties never included filling awkward silences.

I squeezed Percy's arm when we passed the door, a thank you, and Percy pursed his lips and put on a blankness that would have done Modred credit. He knew—at least he reasoned that there was trouble; Percivale was good at thinking, duty fix or no.

We came topside, into that huge formal dining room with the weapons and the real wooden beams and the flickering lights like live flame. All of them who had sat down at table got up again to help serve, excepting Griffin and Dela of course, who sat together at the head of the table. It was a scandalous profusion of food, when we were only then setting up the lab that was, at best, never going to give us delicacies such as this: but Dela was never one to scant herself while the commodity held out—be it lovers or wines or the food we had to live on. Maybe it pleased her vanity to feed her servants so extravagantly; she had brought us to appreciate such things—even Modred was not immune to such pleasures. Perhaps it was humor. Or perhaps it was something more complicated, like flinging her money about like a challenge—even here. Here—because Griffin was here to be impressed.

"Sit, sit down," Dela bade us with a grand wave of her hand, and we did. She had saved Lance the place at her left hand, and me the one at Griffin's right; and then came Gawain and Lynette, Percivale at the end; Vivien and Modred next to Lance. We ate, serving ourselves further helpings. Dela chattered away quite gaily—so beautiful she was, with her pale braids done up beside her face, and her gown cut low to show off her fine fair complexion; and Griffin, blond and handsome beside her . . . they talked of times they had had in the mountains near Brahmani Dali, and of what a bizarre occurrence this was, and how Griffin thought she took it all marvelously well and was very brave.

Nonsense, I thought. Neither one of them was taking it that calmly: *we* saw.

"I have good company," she said. And she patted Griffin's hand on the tabletop and patted Lance's, and I swallowed hard at my wine, having about as much as I could stomach. I unfocused my eyes and looked at the plate. I knew that I ought not to look on Lance's face just then; I gave him that grace.

"Lancelot, and I," Griffin said, "passed time in the gym today. We should meet again tomorrow. It's been a long time since I found a match my size."

"Sir," Lance murmured.

"Not sir," Griffin said. "Not down there. You don't hold back. You really fight. I like that."

"Yes, sir," Lance whispered back.

"Be there tomorrow," Griffin said, "same time."

"Yes, sir," he said again.

Dela looked at Lance suddenly. She was frivolous at times, our lady, but she was not stupid; and she surely knew Lance better than she knew any of us. A frown came over her face and I knew what did it, that meek softness in Lance, that quiet, quiet voice.

There was a little silence in the party, over the taped music, in which Gawain's letting a knife slip against his plate rang devastatingly loud.

"We can't let it get us down," Griffin said. "We're here, that's all; and there's no getting out again; and we're going to live for years."

"Years and years," Dela said, winding her fingers with his. "All of us." She looked on us. "We're—very glad not to be quite alone. You understand that, all of you? I'm very glad to be able to trust my staff. However long we stay here—there's no law here; we've talked about that, Griffin and I: there's no law—no fortieth year. Even if we reach it here. You understand me? We're together in this."

It took a moment, this declaration. It hit my stomach like a fist even when I felt happy about it. A shift like that in the whole expected outcome of my life—it was a change as bizarre as dropping through the hole in space, and demanded its own sensory adjustments. Not to be put down. To live to be old. *Old* was not a territory I had mapped out for myself. I looked at Lance, who looked somewhat as dazed as I, and at the others—at Vivien, who had wanted this for herself and thought she was exclusive in her privilege; at Modred, whose face never yet showed any great excitement, only a flickering about the eyes; at Gawain and Lynette and Percy, who looked back at me in shock.

Of course, I thought, of course my lady needed us. It was insanity for them to put any of us down. They'd be alone then. It made sense.

"Thank you," I said, finding my voice first, and the others murmured something like. It was an eerie thing to say thank you for. Dela smiled benevolently and lifted her glass at us. She was, I think, a little drunk; and so perhaps was Griffin, who had started on the wine when Dela had. Both their faces were flushed. They drank, and we did, to living.

And something hit the ship.

Not hard. It was a tap that rang through the hull and stopped us all, like the stroke of midnight in one of Dela's stories, that froze us where we sat, enchantment ended.

And it came again. Tap. Tap-tap. Tap-tap-tap. Tap-tap-tap-tap.

"O my God," Dela said.

He names himself the Night, and oftener Death,
And wears a helmet mounted with a skull,
And bears a skeleton figured on his arms,
To show that who may slay or scape the three
Slain by himself shall enter endless night.

VI

We ran to the bridge, all of us in a rush, Gawain and
Percy first, being nearest the door, and the rest of us on their
heels, out of breath and frightened out of our minds. The
hammering kept up. Gawain and Lynn slid in at controls,
Percy and Modred took their places down the boards, and
the rest of us—the rest of us just hovered there holding on to
each other and looking at the screens, which showed nothing
different that I could tell.

Modred started doing something at his board, and com
came on very loud, distantly echoing the tapping.

"What are you doing?" Dela asked sharply.

"Listening," Lynette said as the sounds shifted. Other pickups were coming into play. "Trying to figure out just where
they are on the hull."

Dela nodded, giving belated permission, and we all stayed
very quiet while Modred kept sorting through the various
pickups through the ship.

It got loud of a sudden, and very loud. I flinched and tried
not to. It went quiet of a sudden, then loud again, and my
lady Dela swore at Modred.

"Somewhere forward," Modred said with a calm reach that
did something to lower the sound. "About where we touch
the mass."

"Trying to break through," Gawain muttered, "possibly."

"Wayne," Percivale said abruptly, urgently. "I'm getting a pulse on com; same pattern. Response?"

"No!" Dela cried, before ever Gawain could say anything. *"No,* you don't answer it."

"Lady Dela, they may breach us."

"They. They. We don't know what it is."

"He's right," Griffin said. "That *they* out there counts, Dela; and they're trying a contact. If they don't know we're alive in here, they could breach that hull and kill us all—at the least, damage the ship, section by section. And then what do we do?—That area forward," he said to the crew. "Put the emergency seals onto it."

"Presently engaged," Lynn said.

"Don't you give orders," Dela snapped. "Don't you interfere with my crew."

Griffin no more than frowned, but he was doing that already. My lady pushed away from his arm, crossed the deck to stand behind Gawain and Lynn. "Are there arms aboard?" Griffin asked.

"Stop meddling."

"Tapes never prepared your crew for this. How much do you expect of them? Are there weapons aboard? Have they got a block against using them?"

Dela looked about at him, wild. She seemed then to go smaller, as if it were all coming at her too fast. I had never imagined a born-man blanking, but Dela looked close to it. "There aren't any weapons," she said.

The hammering stopped, a dire and thickish silence.

"Are we still getting that signal?" Griffin asked.

"Yes," Percy said after a moment, answering Griffin. It made me shiver, this yes-no of our lady's, standing there, looking like she wanted to forbid, and not. Percy brought the sound from the com up so we could hear it, and it was a timed pulse of static. One. One-two. One-two-three.

"Maybe—" Dela found her voice. "Maybe it's something natural."

"In this place?" Griffin asked. "I think we'd better answer that call. Make it clear we're in here.—Dela, they know, they *know* this ship's inhabited if it's whole: what *are* ships but inhabited? And the question isn't whether they breach that hull; it's how they do it. Silence could be taken for unfriendly intentions. Or for our being dead already, and then they might not be careful at all."

Dela just stared. The static pulses kept on. I held to Lance's arm and felt him shivering too.

"Answer it," Griffin said to Percivale.

"No," Dela said, and Griffin stared at her, frowning, until she made a spidery, resigning motion of her hand.

"Go on," Griffin said to Percivale. "Can you fine it down, get something clearer out of that?"

The whole crew looked round at their places, in Dela's silence. And finally she nodded and shrugged and looked away, an I-don't-care. But she did care, desperately; and I felt sick inside.

"Get to it," Griffin snapped at them. "Before we lose it."

Backs turned. Percy and Modred worked steadily for a few moments, and we started getting a clear tone.

"Answer," Griffin said again, and this time Percy looked around at Dela, and Modred did, slowly and refusing to be hurried.

"Do whatever he says," Dela murmured, her arms wrapped about her as if she were shivering herself. She rolled her eyes up at the screens, but the screens showed us nothing new.

And all of a sudden the com that had been giving out steady tones snapped and sputtered with static. It started gabbling and clicking, not a static kind of click, but a ticking that started in the bass register like boulders rolling together and rumbled up into higher tones until it became a shriek. We all jerked from the last notes, put our hands over our ears: it was that kind of sound. And it rumbled back down again—softer—someone had gotten the volume adjusted— and kept rumbling, slow, slow ticks.

"Not human," Griffin said. "Not anything like it. But then what did we expect? *Send*. Answer in their pattern. See if it changes."

Hands moved on the boards.

"Nothing," Percy said.

Then the com stopped, dead silent.

"Did you cut it?" Griffin asked, ready to be angry.

"It's gone," Modred said. "No pickup now. We're still sending."

The silence continued, eerie after the noise. The ventilation fans seemed loud.

"Kill our signal," Griffin said.

Percy moved his hand on the board, and the whole crew sat still then, with their backs to us, no one moving. I felt Lance's hand tighten on mine and I held hard on to his. We were all scared. We stood there a long time waiting for something . . . anything.

Dela unclasped her arms and turned, flinging them wide in a desperately cheerful gesture. "Well," she said, "they're thinking it over, aren't they? I think we ought to go back down and finish off the drinks."

Her cheer fell flat on the air. "You go on back," Griffin said.

"What more can you do here? It's their move, isn't it? There's no sense all of us standing around up here. Gawain and Modred can keep watch on it. Come on. I want a drink, Griffin."

He looked at her, and he was scared too, was master Griffin. Dela had let him give us orders, and now whatever-it-was knew about us in here. I felt sick at my stomach and probably the rest of us did. Griffin didn't move; and Dela came close to him, which made me tense; and Lance—Griffin might hit her; he had hit me when he was afraid. But she slipped her white arm into his and tugged at him and got him moving, off the bridge. He looked back once. Maybe he sensed our distress with him. But he went with her. Percy and Lynette got up from their places and Lance and Viv and I trailed first after Griffin and my lady, getting them back to the dining hall.

They sat down and drank. We had no invitation, and we cleaned up around them, even Lynette and Vivien, ordinarily above such things, while my lady made a few jokes about what had happened and tried to lighten things. Griffin smiled, but the humor overall was very thin.

"Let's go to bed," my lady suggested finally. "That's the way to take our minds off things."

Griffin thought it over a moment, finally nodded and took her hand.

"The wine," Dela said. "Bring that."

Viv and I brought it, while Lance took the dishes down and Percy and Lynn went elsewhere. My lady and Griffin went to the sitting room to drink, but I went in to turn down the bed, and then collected Vivien and left. We were free to go, because my lady was not as formal with us as she had us be with her guests. Whenever *she* left us standing unnoticed, that meant go.

Especially when she had a man with her. And especially now, I thought. Especially now.

We went back to our quarters, where Lynn and Percy and Lance had gathered, all sitting silent, Lynn and Percy at a game, Lance watching the moves. There was no cheer there.

"Go a round?" I asked Lance. He shook his head, content to watch. I looked at Vivien, who was doing off her clothes and putting them away. No interest there either. I went to the locker and undressed and put on a robe for comfort, and came and sat by Lance, watching Lynn and Percy play. Viv sat down and read—we did have books, of our own type, for idle moments, something to do with the hands and minds, but they were all dull, tame things compared to the tapes, and they were homilies which were supposed to play off our psych-sets and make us feel good. Me, I felt bored with them, and hollow when I read them.

We would live. That change in our fortunes still rose up and jolted me from time to time. No more thought of being put down, no more thinking of white rooms and going to sleep forever; but it was strange—it had no comfort. It gave us something to fear the same as born-men. Maybe we should have danced about the quarters in celebration; but no one mentioned it. Maybe some had forgotten. I think the only thing really clear in our minds was the dread that the horrid banging might start up again at any moment—at least that was the clearest thought in mine: that the hammering might start and the hull might be breached, and we might be face to face with what lived out there. I watched the game board, riveting my whole mind on the silences and the position of the pieces and the sometime moves Lynn and Percy made, predicting what they would do, figuring it out when expectation went amiss. It was far better occupation than the thoughts that gnawed round the edges of my mind, making that safe center smaller and smaller.

The game went to stalemate. We all sat there staring blankly at a problem that could not be resolved—like the one outside—and feeling the certainty settling tighter and tighter over the game, were cheated by it of having *some* sort of an-

swer, to something. Lynn swore, mildly, an affectation aped
from born-men. It seemed overall to be fit.

So the game was done. The evening was. Lance got up,
undressed and went to bed ahead of the rest of us, while Viv
sat in her lighted corner reading. I came and shoved my bed
over on its tracks until it was up against his. Lance paid no
attention, lying on his side with his back to me until I edged
into his bed and up against his back.

He turned over then. "No," he said, very quiet, just the
motion of his lips in the light we had left from Viv's reading,
and the light from the bathroom door. Not a fierce no, as it
might have been. There was pain; and I smoothed his curling
hair and kissed his cheek.

"It's all right," I said. "Just keep me warm."

He shifted over and his arms went about me with a fervent
strength; and mine about him; and maybe the others thought
we made love: it was like that, for a long time, long after all
the lights but Viv's were out. Finally that one went. And then
when we lay apart but not without our arms about each
other, came a giving of the mattress from across Lance's side,
and Vivien lay down and snuggled up to him, not because
she was interested in Lance, but just that we did that sometimes, lying close, when things were uncertain. It goes back to
the farms; to our beginnings; to nightmares of being alone, to
good memories of lying all close together, and touching, and
being touched. It was comfort. It put no demands on
Lance. In a moment more Percivale and Lynette moved a
bed up and lay down there, crowding in on us, so that if
someone had to get up in the night it was going to wake everyone. But all of us, I think, wanted closeness more than we
wanted sleep.

I know I didn't sleep much, and sometimes, in that kind of
glow the ceiling let off when eyes had gotten used to the
dark, I could make out Lance's face. He lay on his back, and
I think he stared at the ceiling, but I could not be sure. I kept
my arm about his; and Percy was at my right keeping me
warm on that side, with Lynette all tangled up with him; and
Viv sleeping on Lance's shoulder on the other side. No sex.
Not at all. All I could think of was that sound: we had fallen
into something that was never going to let us go; we clung
like a parasite to something that maybe didn't want us at-

tached to it at all; and out there . . . out there beyond the hull, if I let my senses go, was still that terrible chaos-stuff.

If this was death, I kept thinking, remembering my lady's mad hypothesis, if this was death, I could wish we had not tangled some other creature up in our dying dream. But I believed now it was no dream, because I could never have imagined that sound out of my direst nightmares.

It came again in the night, that rumbling over com: Gawain came on the intercom telling Percy and Lynn so; and all of us scrambled out of bed and ran for the lift.

So had Griffin come running from my lady's bedroom. He stood there in his robe and his bare feet like the rest of us; but no word from my lady, nothing. It left us with Griffin alone, and that rumbling and squealing came over the com fit to drive us all blank.

"Have you answered it?" Griffin asked of Gawain and Modred, who sat at controls still in their party clothes; and Percy and Lynn took their places in their chairs wearing just the robes they had thrown on. "No," Modred replied. He turned in his place, calm as ever, with dark circles under his eyes. "I'm composing a transmission tape in pulses, to see if we can establish a common ground in mathematics."

"Use it," Griffin said. "If the beginning's complete, use it."

Modred hesitated. I stood there with my arms wrapped about me and thinking, no, he wouldn't, not with my lady not here. But Modred gave one of those short, curious nods of his and pushed a button.

The transmission went out. At least after a moment the transmission from the other side stopped. "I should see to my lady," I said.

"No," Griffin said. "She's resting. She took a pill."

I stood there as either/or as Modred, clenched my arms about me and let this born-man tell me I wasn't to go . . . because I knew if my lady had taken a pill she wouldn't want the disturbance. This terrible thing started up again and the crew asked help and Dela took a pill.

An arm went about me. It was Lance. Viv sat near us, on one of the benches near the door.

"You'd better trade off shifts," Griffin said to the crew, marking, surely, how direly tired Gawain and Modred looked.

"Yes," Gawain agreed. He would have sat there all the

watch if Griffin hadn't thought of that, which was one of the considerate things I had seen Griffin do . . . but it gave me no comfort, and no comfort to any of the rest of us, I think. It was Dela who should have thought of that; Dela who should be here; and it was Griffin instead, who started acting as if he owned us and the *Maid*. Until now he had looked through us all and ignored us; and now he saw us and we were alone with him.

"We'll dress," Lynn said, "and come up and relieve you."

"Get back to sleep," Griffin said to those of us who were staff. "No need of your being here."

We went back to the crew quarters and got in bed again, except Lynn and Percy, who dressed and went topside again. Then Gawain and Modred came down and undressed and lay down with us as Lynn and Percy had—I think they were glad of the company, and worked themselves up against us, cold and tense until they began to take our warmth, and until they fell asleep with the suddenness of exhaustion.

What went on out there, that noise, that thing outside our hull—it might go on again and again. It might not need to sleep.

The huge pavilion slowly yielded up,
Thro' those black foldings, that which housed therein.
High on a nightblack horse, in nightblack arms,
With white breastbone, and barren ribs of Death,
And crowned with fleshless laughter—some ten steps—
Into the half-light—thro' the dim dawn—advanced
The monster, and then paused, and spake no word.

VII

We went about in the morning on soft feet and small steps, listening. We stayed to our duties, what little of them there were. Even the makeshift lab was quiet, where Vivien was setting things up . . . running tests, that took time, and we could do nothing there. Griffin and Dela stayed together in her bed, and I walked and paced feeling like a ghost in the *Maid's* corridors, all too conscious how vast it was outside and how small we were and how huge that rumbling voice had sounded.

"It's probably trapped here too," Dela said when I came finally to do her hair, "and maybe it's as scared as we are."

"Maybe it is," I said, thinking that scared beasts bit; and I feared this one might have guns. On the *Maid* we had only the ancient weapons which decorated her dining hall and the lady's quarters and some of the corridors. Precious good *those* were against this thing. I thought about knights and dragons and reckoned that they must have been insane.

I finished my lady's hair . . . made it beautiful, elaborate with braids, and dressed her in her green gown with the pale green trim. It encouraged me, that she was up and sober again, no longer lying in her chambers prostrate with fear: if my lady could face this day, then things might be better. If there was an answer to this, then born-men could find it; and she was our born-man, ours, who dictated all the world.

"Where's Griffin?" she asked.

"It's eleven hundred hours. Master Griffin—asked Lance—"

"I remember." She waved her hand, robbed me of the excuse I had hoped for to stop all of that, dismissing it all.

"Shall I go?" I asked.

Again a wave of the hand. My lady walked out into the sitting room and sat down at the console there, started calling up something on the comp unit—all the log reports, I reckoned, of all the time she had slept; or maybe the supply inventories. My lady was herself again; and let Griffin beware.

I padded out, ever so quietly, closed the door and wiped my hands and headed down the corridor to the lift as fast as I could walk. I went down and toward the gym in the notion that I had to be quiet, but quiet did no good at all: the gym rang with the impact of feet and bodies. They were at it again, Griffin and Lance, trying to throw each other.

It was crazy. They were. I had thought of lying again, saying that Dela wanted this or that, but she was paying sharp attention today, and the lie would not pass. I stood there in the doorway and watched.

They were at it this time, I reckoned, because there had been no decision the last encounter, thanks to me. No winner; and Griffin wanted to win—had to win, because Lance was lab-born, and shouldn't win, shouldn't even be able to contest with the likes of Griffin.

They went back and forth a great deal, muscles straining, skin slick with sweat that dampened their hair and made their hands slip. Neither one could get the advantage standing; and they hit the floor with a thud and neither one could get the other stopped. They didn't see me, I don't think. I stood there biting my lip until it hurt. And suddenly it was Lance on the bottom, and Griffin slowly let him up.

I turned away, fled the doorway for the corridor, because I was ashamed, and hurt, and I didn't want to admit to myself why, but it was as if I had lost too, like it was my pain, that Lance after all proved what we were made to be, and that we always had to give way. Even when he did what none of the rest of us could do, something so reckless as to fight with Griffin—he was beaten.

Lance came up to the crew quarters finally, where I sat playing solitaire. He was undamaged on the outside, and I tried to act as if I had no idea anything was wrong, as if I had never been in that doorway or seen what I had seen. But I reckoned that he wanted to have his privacy now, so downcast his look was, and I could hardly walk out without seeming to avoid him, so I curled up on the couch and pretended to be tired of my game, to sleep awhile.

But I watched him through my lashes, as he rummaged in his locker, and found a tape, and set up the machine. He took the drug, and lay down in deepsleep, lost in that; and all the while I had begun to know what tape it was, and what he was doing, and what was into him. The understanding sent cold through me.

He should not be alone. I was sure of that. The lady had deserted him and his having the tape in the first place was my fault. I took the drug and set up the connections, and lay down beside him in his dream—lay down with my fingers laced in his limp ones and began to slip toward it.

The story ran to its end and stopped, letting us out of its grip; and whether he felt me there or not, he just lay there with tears streaming from his closed eyes. Finally I couldn't stand it any longer and took the sensors off him and me and put my arms about him.

But he mistook what I wanted and pushed me away, stared at the ceiling and blanked awhile.

It was that bad.

And when he came out of it he said nothing, but got up, went to the bath and washed his face and left. Me, who was so long his friend, he left without a word. I heard the lift go down again; and it was the galley or the gym down there, so I had no difficulty finding him.

It was the gym. From the door I watched him . . . doing pushups until I thought his arms must break, as if it could drive the weakness out of him.

Now, Beast, I thought toward the voice that had terrorized our night. Now, if ever you have something to say. But it stayed mute. Lance struggled against his own self; and I wished with all my heart that someone would discover some duty for him, some use that would get him busy.

He saw me there, turning suddenly. I knew he did by his scowl when he got to his feet, and I turned and fled down the corridor, to the lift, to the upper level, as far from the gym as I could excepting Viv's domain.

And came Percivale, down the corridor from the bridge, looking as dispirited as I felt.

"Percy," I said, catching at his arm. "Percy, I want you to do something for me."

"What?" he asked, blinking at my intense assault; and I explained I wanted him to go down to the gym and fight with Lance. "It's good for you," I said, "because we don't know what's out there trying to get in, do we? and you might have to fight, to protect the ship and the lady. I think it's a good idea to be ready. Griffin's been working out with Lance. I'm sure it would be good for all of you."

Percy thought about that, ran a hand over his red hair. "I'll talk to Gawain and Modred," he said. "But Lance is much stronger than we are."

"But you should try," I said, "at least try. Lance did, with Griffin, with a born-man, after all; and can't you, with him?"

Percivale went down there first, and later that afternoon the three of them were looking the worse for wear and there was a little brighter look in Lance's eyes when I saw him at dinner. I smiled smugly across the table in the great hall, next Griffin and my lady, with all the table set as it had been the evening before, and all of us again in our party best.

"I think it's given up," my lady said, quite cheerful, lifting her glass.

It was true. There had been silence all day. Modred was glum. His carefully constructed tapes had failed. Gawain said so . . . and my lady laughed, a brave, lonely sound.

Griffin smiled a faint, small quirk of the lips, more courtesy than belief. And drank his wine. Before dinner was done something did ring against the hull, a vague kind of thump; and the crew started from their places, and Griffin did.

"*No!*" my lady snapped, stopping the crew on the instant, and Griffin, half out of his chair, hesitated. "We can't be running at every shift and settling," Dela said. "Sit down! The lot of you sit down. It's nothing."

My heart felt it would break my ribs. But no further sound came to us, and the crew settled back into their places and Griffin sat back down.

"We would have felt a settling," Griffin said.

"Enough of it. Enough."

There was silence for a moment, no movement, all down the table; but my lady set to work on her dessert, and Griffin did, and so did we all. My lady talked, and Griffin laughed, and soon we all talked again, even Lance, idle dinner chatter. I took it for a sign of health in Lance, that I might have done some good, and I felt my own spirits higher for it. Dela and master Griffin finished their meal, we took the dishes down, and Lance remained tolerably cheerful when we were in the galley together. He was smiling, if not overly talkative.

But it didn't help that night. Lance was sore and full of bruises, and he wanted to be let alone. He didn't object to my moving my bed over or getting in with him, but he turned his back on me, and I patted his shoulder. Finally he turned an anguished look on me in the light there was left in the room, with the others lying in their beds. He started to say something. He didn't need to. I just lay still and took his hand in mine, and he put his arm about me and stroked my hair, with that old sadness in his eyes, stripped of anger. I could hear noises from farther over toward the wall, where Lynn slept. Either Gawain or Percy had come somewhat off the duty fix, and presumably so had Lynette.

Misery, I thought. And Lance just lay there in the dark looking at me.

"It happens to born-men too," I said. I knew that, and maybe he didn't. He had been more sheltered, in his way. "They're more complicated than we are, and they get this a lot, this trouble; but they get over it."

He shivered, and I knew he was caught somewhere in his own psych-sets, where I couldn't truly help him, and he wasn't about to discuss it. There was no *reason* for Lance, I thought. The lady and Griffin, and when it turned out that this voyage wasn't ending, ever, then that was it for Lancelot, done, over. He cared for nothing else in all existence but my lady; and when he was shut away from her, that was when he—

—heard the story in the tape, and learned what the mean-

ing of my lady's fancy was, and what he was named for, and
he began to dream of being that dream of hers. That thought
came to me while we lay there in the dark. And there was a
great hollowness in me, knowing that. Lance had found himself a kind of purpose, but I had nothing like his, that
touched his central psych-sets. Being just Elaine, a minor
player in the tape, I was meant to do nothing but keep Lance
entertained when my lady was otherwise occupied, and to do
my lady's hair and to look decorative, and nothing more,
nothing more.

Our purposes are always small. We're small people, pale
copies, filled with tapes and erasable. But something had begun to burn in Lance that had more complicated reasons; and
I was afraid—not for myself, not really for myself, I kept
reasoning in my heart, although that was part of my general
terror. We should live as long as we liked. The lady had
promised us, ignoring that thing out there, ignoring the uncertainties which had settled on us . . . like growing old. Like
our minds growing more and more complicated just by living,
until we grew confused beyond remedy. We were promised
life. The thing out there in the dark, the chaos waiting whenever we might grow confused enough to let our senses slip
back into the old way of seeing—this living with death so
close to us, was that different than our lives ever were? And
didn't born-men themselves live that way, when they deliberately took chances?

It was just that our death talked to us through the hull,
had called us on com, had tapped the hull this evening just to
let us know that he was still there. *Death,* not an erasing; not
the white room where they take you at the end.

We're already dying, my lady had insisted once; and my
mind kept wandering back to that. I looked into Lance's troubled eyes and smiled, thinking that at least we were going to
die like born-men, and have ourselves a fight with our Death,
like in the fables.

Thermopylae. Roland at the pass. When it got to us we
would blow the horns and meet it head on. But that was in
the fables.

I began to think of other parts of the story, Lancelot's part,
how he had to be brave and be the strongest of all.

And of what the rest of us must be.

Lance slept for a while, and I snuggled up under his chin and slept too, happy for a while, although I couldn't have said why . . . something as inexplicable as psych-set, except that it was a nice place to be, and I found it strange that even in his sleep he held onto me, not the closeness we take for warmth, and far from sex too . . . just that it was nice, and it was something—

—like in the tape, I thought. I wondered who I was to him. I reckoned I knew. And being only Elaine, I took what small things I could get. Even that gave me courage. I slept.

Then the hammering started again on the hull.

I tensed, waking. Lance sat up, and we held onto each other, while all about us the others were waking too. It wasn't the patterned hammering we had heard before. It came randomly and loud.

Gawain piled out of bed and the rest of us were hardly slower, excepting Vivien, who sat there clutching her sheet to her chest in the semidark and looking when the lights came on as if it was all going to be too much for her.

But she moved, grabbed for her clothes and started dressing. Modred was out the door first, and Percy after him; and Gawain and Lynette right behind them. Lance and I stopped at least to throw our clothes on and then ran for it, leaving Viv to follow as she could.

We ran, the last bit from the lift, breathless, down the corridor to the bridge. The crew had found their places. My lady and Griffin were there, both in their robes, and my lady at least looked grateful that we two had shown up. I went and gave her my hand, and Lance stood near me—not that presumptuous, not with one of my lady's lovers holding the other.

"They say it's the same place as before," Dela informed us as Vivien showed up and delayed by the door. "But it doesn't sound like a signal."

It sounded like someone working on the other side of the hull, to me. Tap. Bang. And long pauses.

The crew was talking frantically among themselves— Modred and Percy answering questions from Lynn and Gawain, making protests. Griffin let go my lady's hand and walked into that half U near them, leaning on the back of Percy's chair.

Only my lady Dela stood there shivering, and went over to a bench and sat down. I sat down and put my arms about her, and Lance hovered helplessly by while I tried to keep her warm in her nightgown. She was crying. I had never seen Dela cry like this. She was scared and trembling and it was contagious.

"Give us vid," Griffin was saying. "Let's see if we can't figure out what happened to the rest of the ships around us. See if they're breached in some way."

Vid came on, all measled red and glare, shading off to greens and purples where some object was. "Forward floods," Modred said "Wayne."

"Just let it alone," Dela snapped. "Let it be. If we start turning the lights on and looking round out there we'll encourage it."

Modred stopped. So did Gawain.

"Do it," Griffin said. And when they did nothing: "Dela, what are we going to do, wait for it?"

"That's all we can do, isn't it?"

"It's not all I choose to do. We're going to fight that thing if it has to be."

"For what good?"

"Because I'm not sitting here waiting for it."

"And you encourage it and it gets to us—"

"We still have a chance when we know it's coming.—Put the floods on," he said to Gawain.

Gawain looked at Dela. "We think the sound is coming from inside the wheel . . . not one of the smaller ships: from where we contact the torus."

Dela just shivered where she sat, between us; and Viv hovered near the door, frozen.

"Dela," Griffin said, "go on back to bed. Give the order and go back to bed. Nothing's going to happen. We look and get some clear images of where it's coming from, that's all."

Dela gave the order, a wave of her hand. The floods went on and played over blacknesses that were other ships. We sat staring into that black and red chaos, at ships bleeding light through their wounds. Dela turned her face into my shoulder and I locked my arms about her as tightly as I could, stared helplessly into that place that I remembered of a sudden, that chaos senses had to forget the moment it stopped. I turned my face away from it, looked up at Lance's face which was as chaos-lost as I felt; and Viv, Vivien holding on to the door. It was hard to look back again, and harder not to. Griffin was still giving orders—had the cameras sweep this way and that, and there was that ship next to us, the delicate one like spiderweb; and a strange one on our other side, that we had slid up against when we were grappling on; we couldn't see all of it. And mostly the view dissolved in that red bleeding light. But when the cameras centered on our own bow, we could almost see detail, like it was lost in a wash of light across the lens, something that was like machinery. A cold feeling was running through my veins. "I don't remember our nose like that," I said. No one paid attention to me.

"See if you can fine it down now," Griffin said. "What happened to your last setup on that?"

"Everything's shifted," Modred said. I hoped he meant the figures.

Griffin swore and turned away, paced the floor. Maybe it was hard for him to stare at the screens for any length of time. I know it got to my stomach; and even the crew looked uncomfortable, jolted out of sleep, with that terrible banging never ceasing. Tap. Bang. Bang. Tap-tap-tap.

Lynette turned around at her place. "We might ungrapple," she offered, looking at Dela, not Griffin. "We can push off and disrupt whatever they're doing on the other side."

"*Do* it," Dela said, snatched at that with all the force in her. Griffin looked like he wanted to say something and shut his mouth instead. Lynn turned about again, all coolly done. She touched switches and boards came alight.

"Take hold," Percy warned us. We hurried and got Dela and Griffin to the emergency cushions, got ourselves snugged in, Viv first, and Lance and myself together, holding hands for comfort.

Moving would delay things. It would give us time. But maybe the thing out there had guns, I thought; maybe when we moved it would just start shooting and all we would have of life would be just the next moment, when the fragile *Maid* was blown apart.

Did Lynn and the others think of that? Was that what Griffin had almost said? Maybe my listening to his tapes, all those things about wars and killing people, let me think such things. I felt like I was sweating all the way to my insides.

The crew talked to each other. It took them forever . . .

judging, I guessed, how hard and how far and what we were going to grab to next that might make it harder for whatever was trying to hammer through our bow. Finally:

"Stand by," Lynette said.

And Vivien answer'd frowning yet in wrath:
"O ay; what say ye to Sir Lancelot, friend,
Traitor or true? that commerce with the Queen,
I ask you. . . ."

VIII

It came simultaneously, the clang of the grapples disconnecting, the shudder that might be our engines working.

"Shut it down," Percy cried. "Shut it down!"

"No," Lynn said, and the shuddering kept up, like out-of-tune notes quavering through metal frame and living bone. Lynn reached suddenly across the board. The harmonics stopped. Gawain, beside her, made a move and the grapples slammed on again.

"We didn't move," Dela said softly; and louder: "We didn't move."

Lynn swung her chair about. "No." There was thorough anguish on her freckled face. "Something's got a grapple on *us*. We can't break it loose."

"Do it!" Dela was unbuckling the restraints. She got them undone as the rest of us got out of ours. She stood up and thrust Griffin's hand off when he got up and tried to put his hand on her shoulder. "You find a way to do it."

"Lady Dela, we already took a chance with it."

"Listen to your captains," Griffin said, taking Dela's shoulders and refusing this time to be shaken off. "Listen. Will you listen to what she's trying to tell you?"

"We didn't move at all," Lynn said, with soft, implacable precision. "Our own grapples went back on right where they had been, to the millimeter. We gave it repulse straight on and angled and we didn't shake it even that much. That's a solid hold they've got on us."

"Well, why did you let them get it on us?" Dela's voice went brittle. "Why did you play games with it and let this happen?"

"Last night at dinner," Modred said in his ordinary, flat voice, "we should have investigated. But it was probably too late."

Only Modred was that nerveless, to turn something back at Dela. She cursed him, and all of us, and Griffin, and told him to let her go. He didn't and Modred never flinched.

"They've told you the truth," Griffin said, making her look at him: there was no one but Lance could fight back against a strength like Griffin had; but he let her go when she struck at his arms, and stood there when she hit him hard in the chest in her temper. And we stood there—I, and Lance— even Lance, watching this man put hands on Dela, because somehow he had gotten round to Lynn's side, and Modred's and the ship's, and we were standing with him, not understanding how it was happening to us.

Maybe Dela realized it too. She made a throwaway gesture, turned aside, not looking at anyone. "Go on," she said. "Go on. Do what you like. You have all the answers."

She stayed that way, facing no one, her hands locked in front of her. Griffin stared at her as if she had set him at a loss, like all of us were. Then he looked over at us. "Get her out," he said quietly. "All of you who don't have to be here, out. Crew too: offshirt crew, go back to sleep. This may go on into the next watch. We have to put up with it."

I didn't know what to do for the moment. I wasn't supposed to take his orders about my lady Dela, but then, Dela was fit to say something if she wanted to say something. I hesitated. Lance did, not included in that order, things being as they were. "Come," I said then, and went and hugged Dela against me. "Come on."

Dela put her arms about me, seeming suddenly small and uncertain, and I put mine about her and led her back through the corridor to her own rooms. Then she walked on her own, in her own safe sitting-room, but I held her hand, because she seemed to want that, and led her back into her own bedroom and did off her shoes and her robe and tucked her into that big soft blue bed. She was still shivering . . . my brave, my strong-minded lady. Just last evening she had put courage into us, had talked to us and made us sit down and almost made us believe it would all turn out. She had made herself believe it too, I think; and it was all unraveling.

Vivien had followed us . . . not Lance. He had not felt permitted, or he would have. "Get her a drink," I told Viv—when she could hardly round on me and tell me to do it myself; she gave me a black hysterical look and went over to the sideboard. I sat with my lady and kept my arm about her behind the pillow. The banging at the hull began again, and Dela's hands were clenched whitely on the bedclothes.

"It can't get in," I offered, not believing it myself any longer. "Or it would have done it already. It's just wishing, that's all."

Vivien brought the wine. Dela took it in both hands and drank, and seemed to feel better after half a glass. Vivien sat down on the other side of the wide mattress and I stayed where I was, just being near Dela. For a long time Dela drank in small sips, and stared with detached interest at some place before her, while the hammering kept up.

"Go on," my lady said finally, to Vivien. "Go on." But she didn't look at me when she said it, and when Vivien got up and left, I stayed. "Get me another drink," she asked quite calmly. "I can't stand that noise."

I did so, and took one for myself, because alone, we were not on formalities.

And I sat there beside her while she was on her second glass, my hand locked in hers. Psych-set: Dela was hurting, above and beyond the fear; I could sense that. A frown creased her brow. Her blonde hair fell about her lace-gowned shoulders and she leaned there among the lacy pillows drinking the wine and looking oddly young.

"Why doesn't he come back?" she asked of me, as if I should know what born-men thought. "We're stuck here. Why can't he accept that?"

"Maybe he thinks he could beat it."

She shook her head, a cascade of pale blonde among the pillows. "No. He doesn't." She freed her hand of mine and changed hands with the wineglass, patted Griffin's accustomed place in the huge bed. "He's so good to me. He tried so hard to be brave, and I know he's scared, because he's young—that's not rejuv: that's his real age. He doesn't know much. Oh, he's traveled a bit, but not like this." A soft, desperate laugh, as if she had realized her own bad joke. A reknitting of the brows. "He's scared. And he doesn't have to be nice, but he is, and I do love him, Elaine. He's the first one of all of them who ever didn't have to be nice to me, and he is, and I hate that it has to be him in this mess with us."

I looked desperately at my lap, at my fingers laced there, not liking this business of being dragged into born-man confidence. But we're like the walls. Born-men can talk to us and know our opinion's nothing, so it's rather like talking to themselves. Sold on, we're erased; and here—here where we were, there was no selling, and no gossiping elsewhere, that was certain.

"He's good," Dela said. "You understand that? He's just a good man."

I remembered that he had hit me, but maybe he hadn't seen me right, and he had been scared then. Hitting made no difference to me. Others had hit me. I held no grudges; that wasn't in my psych-set either.

"I'm seventy," Dela said, still talking to me and the walls at once. "And do you know why he's with me? Because we started out as allies to do a little bending of government rules . . . because the government . . . but it doesn't matter. Nothing back there matters. His family; my estates—it doesn't matter at all. There's just that *thing* out there, and I wish he'd leave it alone, let it take its time.—Does dying frighten you, Elaine? Do you ever think about things like that?"

I nodded, though I didn't know if I thought of it the way she meant. She changed hands again and reached and stroked my hair. "Griffin and I . . . you know there are people who don't think you ought to exist at all—that the whole system that made you is wrong. But you value your life, don't you?"

"Yes."

"Griffin and I talked about it. Once. When it mattered. It doesn't now. I meant what I said. We share everything, Griffin and I and all of you, all the food, everything, as long as there's anything. That's the way it is."

"Thank you," I said. What could I say? She had frightened me badly and healed it all at once, and I put my arms about her, really grateful—but I knew better than to think they wouldn't think on it again sometime that things really did run short. I knew my lady Dela, that she had high purposes, and she meant to be good, but as with her lovers and her hopes, sometimes she and her high purposes had fallings-out.

The hammering, dim a moment, suddenly crashed out louder and louder. Dela rolled her eyes at the wooden beams overhead and looked as if she could not bear it. She slammed the empty glass down on the bedside table and scrambled out of bed in a flurry of gowns and blonde hair, on her way back to the intercom in the sitting-room.

"Griffin," I heard her say over the hammering on the hull. I took up her wineglass and refilled it, trembling somewhat, expecting temper when Griffin was Griffin and refused.

"Dela," he answered after a time.

"Griffin, stop it up there and let it alone and come back down here."

"Dela," I heard, standing stock-still and holding my breath. "Dela, there's no waiting for this thing. Modred and I have something. There're *tubes,* Dela, tubes going to all those ships we can see. We don't know what or why, but we're trying to get them a little clearer."

"What good is it to see it? *Modred,* Modred, let it all be, shut it down and let it be."

"Let them alone!" Griffin snapped back. "They're doing a job up here. Do you want me to come down there and explain it all or do you trust me? I thought we had this out. I thought we had an agreement, Dela."

There was long silence, and I clenched my hands together, because there was no one born who talked to Dela Kirn that way, no one.

"All right," Dela said in an unhappy voice. There was a sudden silence, then another tap, very soft, that ran from the hull through my nerves. "All right. Modred, help him. All of you, work with Griffin."

She came back into the bedroom then, and for a moment instead of the youth the rejuv preserved, I saw age, in the slump of her shoulders and the gesture that reached for the doorway as if she had trouble seeing it. I started to go and help her; and then I froze, because I felt wrong in seeing such a thing. She was wounded and sometimes in her wounds she was dangerous. She might hit me. I resigned myself to that when she let go the door and came near, her hand stretched out for me. I took it and set her down on the bedside.

No violence. She began to crawl beneath the covers and I tucked her in and sat down again on the bed, because she had not yet dismissed me. She lifted a hand and patted my cheek, with a mournful look in her blue eyes.

"You'll do what Griffin says too," she said.

"Yes," I said, "if you ask me to."

"I do." She stroked the side of my cheek with her finger as if she were touching statuary. "You're special, you know that. Special, and beautiful, and maybe I shouldn't tangle up your minds the way I have, but you're people, aren't you? You understand loyalty. Or is it all programming?"

"I don't know how to answer," I said, and I was afraid, because it was a terrible kind of question, having my lady delve into my programming and my logic. There were buttons she could push, oh, not physical ones, but real all the same, keys she had that could turn me frozen or, I suspected, hurt me beyond all telling—the key instructions to all my psych-sets. "I could never know if I felt what you feel. But I know I want to take care of you. And I'm very glad it's you and not someone else, lady Dela."

"You think so?"

"I've met others and their owners, and I know how good you really are to us. And if it doesn't offend you, thank you for being good to us all our lives."

Her lips trembled. Outside the hull the hammering still continued, like someone fixing pipes, and she pulled me to her, my face between her hands, and kissed me on the brow.

It touched me in a strange way, like pulling strings that were connected to something deep and connected to everything else. Psych-sets. It's a very pleasurable thing to fulfill a Duty, one of the really implanted ones. And this made me feel I had.

I sat back and she just stared at me a time and kept her hand on mine, as if my being there mattered to her.

"Griffin is a *good man*," she insisted when I had never argued; and there was that frightened look in her eyes.

I reckoned then for once Dela was up against something she just didn't want to think about, just as she tried to believe us all dead when it began to go wrong. This wasn't like the Dela who ran the house on Brahman, who built cities. Then she was all business and hard-minded and no one could say no to her; but now she had no inclination to go running up to the bridge to take command. She might have fought. She abdicated. Griffin showed himself more competent with the ship . . . at least knowing how to talk to the crew. We hadn't defended her. I think that hurt her deeply.

Watch yourself, said I to Griffin, absent. Watch yourself, born-man, when you begin to take the *Maid* away from my lady.—But she had already lost it; and maybe it was that which had so broken Dela's spirit, that the *Maid* which had been so beautiful and so free, which had been Dela Kirn herself in some strange metaphysical connection . . . was held here and smashed and broken, and now threatened with further erosions. I perceived pain, and held to Dela's hand, minded to go on pouring her drinks and to stay here until she could sleep, whatever the infernal hammering meant out there.

I mean, Dela had never cared for the running of the ship, just that it did run, and she had bought Gawain and the others and they were good, the very best: that was her pride. Her money bought the best and it worked and she gave the orders and the ship ran . . . all magical. She had not the least idea how it all worked, far less idea than I did, who lived with the crew. And now Griffin, who claimed to do a little piloting himself insystem . . . just walked in and took them over; and Dela couldn't fight any longer. We were pinned here . . . I think that was the most horrible thing to her, that whatever we did, however we fought, there was never any hope, and while that was true, she had no spirit left at all.

"Call Lance," she said.

My heart stopped. I opened my mouth to babble some excuse on his behalf: he can't, he can't, I thought; but there was no excuse that would hide the truth, and perhaps—perhaps with her—I nodded, rose and went out to the com, pushed 21, the crew quarters. "Lance," I said. "Lance."

"Yes?" the answer came.

"My lady wants you in her quarters."

A silence. "Yes," he said plainly. It was all that had to be said. And very quietly I slipped away out the door, because all that I could do was done.

O Griffin, I thought, you never walk out on my lady; you didn't know that. But you will. And more than that, you're doing things your own way, and she'll never bear with that, not where it touches the *Maid*. Not in that.

But for Lance—for him I was mortally afraid.

I didn't want to go down the lift. I might meet Lance there, coming up, and that was not a meeting I wanted. The knell still rang against the hull, insane hammering that grew loud and soft by turns. I avoided the lift, kept to the main corridor, that took me back to the vicinity of the bridge, where I was not supposed to be, by Griffin's order.

Viv was there, just standing, where she could see in the open door, her hands locked together in an attitude of worry. I startled her, being there, and she scowled and looked back to the bridge.

"What are they up to?" I asked.

"What would you know?" she said. That was Viv. Her old self, worried as she was.

I edged up into the doorway. The main screen was off, but they had a clear image on some. I stood there and stared at our neighbors.

Tubes. Tubes, Griffin had said, and there were, everywhere. At every point a wreck contacted the wheel, the station, whatever it was that had snared us . . . tubes like some kind of obscene parasites that sucked the life from them. Tubes between the ships, as if the growth had pierced them and kept going. The wounds I had thought to have seen, holes in the ships themselves through which the light bled . . . some of those were not: some of those holes had been the arch of those tubes, against the chaos-stuff that was measled black in the still picture. They wre huge, those structures, big enough for access, and irregular in their shapes, like many-branched snakes, like veins and arteries growing out of this thing we had snuggled up to and growing us to its body.

It didn't take much guesswork now to know what was proceeding out there with all those noises. Or why we were stuck fast. There's a thing I'd seen on vid, an access box, and they use it when there's some emergency . . . Hobson's Bridge, I had heard it named. It's a tube and two very powerful pressure gates; and they use it in shipboard disasters when ships have to be boarded and suits aren't sufficient to get people off. You rig it at one side and ride it across; you lock on with the magnetic grapple and you make the seal. You cut through. You're in.

Sometimes I wished I listened to fewer tapes.

Griffin had looked around. He caught me in the doorway, fixed me with that mad blue-eyed stare of his. "Elaine. Did Dela send you?"

"She dismissed me, sir."

He nodded, in a way that more or less accepted my presence there. I took a tentative step inside. Noticed by a born-man, one doesn't vanish when his back is turned. Griffin walked the length of the U at controls, stopped by Modred and looked back again at me. "You understand what we've got here?"

I swallowed against the tightness in my throat and nodded. "Yes, sir."

"How's Dela taking this?"

She had told me to take Griffin's orders, even if she really didn't want me to; and I stood confused, not knowing what I owed where; but I'm high-order, and I don't blank in choices. "I think she's scared, sir; and I don't think she wants to think about it for a while."

That at least was the truth; and it kept Lance out of it. I didn't want Griffin dashing back there to comfort Dela, not now, no.

Griffin ran a hand through his pretty golden hair, and he leaned standing against the chair absent Percy used, looking mortally tired. I felt sorry for him then, and I was not in the habit of feeling sorry for Griffin. He was trying. He had sent Lynn and Percy to rest; and Lance and Viv . . . even if no one was able to. He tried to solve this thing. So did the crew . . . fighting for the *Maid,* even if Dela saw no hope in it.

"You know what a Bridge is?" he asked. "Ship to ship?"

I nodded.

"And Dela—what does she say?"

"Nothing," I said. "But she would understand if she saw that."

He looked still very tired. Looked around at all of us, Gawain and Modred, and back to me. "You're good," he said. "You're very good."

I made a kind of bow of the head, pleased to be told that, even by a stranger. We knew our worth; but it was still good to hear.

"What they're doing," Griffin said, and all at once I was conscious that the hammering had stilled for a while, "is linking into all those ships. That means that something's been alive and doing that a long, long time."

"Yes, sir," I said, contemplating the age of those ships that had come here before us. I looked round the control center, a nervous gesture, missing the sound. "It doesn't take long to set up a Bridge, does it?"

"No," Griffin said. "But I daresay they're jury-rigging. They. It. We have to do something to stop it. You understand that. When you talk to Dela—" He spoke very, very softly, in conspiracy. "When you talk to her, believe that. Protest it in her ear. For her sake. It's your duty, isn't it?—Where's Lance?"

I must have flinched. "Below, sir." We can lie, in duty. He looked at me—he could not have suspected when he asked that question; me, with my face—he had to suspect something behind that flinching, had to think, and know why one of us would lie, and for whom.

"When you see him," he said, ever so quietly, only that tired look on his face, "tell him I'll see the whole staff up here at 1000 this morning. I want to talk to all of you at once. And keep it quiet. I don't want to frighten Dela. You understand that."

I nodded. He walked away to himself, his hands locked behind him, and stopped and looked at the screens. I stood there, while Modred and Gawain consulted and did things with the comp that showed up in the image on the screens.

It looked uglier and uglier, defined, where before the bleeding smears of light had masked all detail. It took on colors, greens and blues. Finally Griffin walked over to the side and looked at Gawain and Modred. "You've got that inventory search run."

"Yes," Modred said, and reached and picked up a handful of printout. Griffin took it. The hammering started again, and even Modred reacted to it, a human glance at the walls about us. Griffin swore, shook his head.

"Go get some rest," he told them. "I'm doing the same."

He started away then, and I moved out of the doorway, to show respect when a born-man wanted past. My heart was beating very fast: com, I was thinking, I could get to com before Griffin could get to Dela's rooms; I could think of something casual to say—something; but Griffin delayed, fixed me with a strangely sad look. "I'm going back to *my* quarters," Griffin said.

I felt my face go hot. I stood there, he walked out, and I didn't make the call. I walked down the corridor after him, headed my own way, for the lift that would take me down to the crew quarters.

Vivien trailed after me, maybe the others too; but I watched Griffin's broad back, his shoulders bowed as if he were very tired, his head down, and for a moment he looked so like Lance in one of his sorrows that I found myself hurting for him.

I knew pain when I saw it. Remember . . . it's my function.

I wished I might go to him, might balance things, set it all right by magic. I walked faster, to overtake him; but my nerve failed me, with the thought that I had no instruction from Dela, and I could not side against her. Not twice. I stopped, close by the lift, and Viv pushed the button, opening the door.

Tap, the sound came against the hull. Tap-bang.

IX

We filed into the crew quarters, Gawain and Modred, Vivien and I . . . quietly as we could, but Lynn and Percy lifted their heads from their pillows all the same. We started taking off boots, settling down for a little rest.

"Where's Lance?" Gawain asked, all innocent.

"Dela called," I said, from my cot where I had lain down next Lance's vacant one; and Gawain's face took on an instant apprehension of things. Viv looked up from taking off her stockings. I closed my eyes and folded my hands on my middle, uncommunicative, trying to shut out the sound from the hull. It was down to a familiar pattern now . . . tap-tap-tap. It grew fainter. I thought of the tubes like branching arteries. Maybe they were working somewhere farther up, at some branching. I imagined such a thing growing over the *Maid*, a basketry of veins, wrapping us about. I shuddered and tried to think of something pleasant. About the dinner table with the artificial candles aglow up and down it, dark wood set with lace and crystal and loaded with fine food and wines. I would like a glass right now, I thought. There were times when I would have gone to the gallery and stolen a bottle. I didn't feel I should. Share and share alike, my lady had said; and the good wine was a thing we would run out of.

Supposing we lasted long enough.

There was silence. I opened my eyes.

"It stopped," Percy said, very hushed.

"Whatever they're doing," Modred said, "they'll have it done sooner or later. I'm only surprised it's taken this long."

"Stop it," Vivien said, very sharp, sitting upright on her bed, and I rolled over to face them, distressed by Viv's temper. "If you'd done your jobs," Viv said, "we wouldn't be in this mess. And if you did something instead of sit and talk about it we might get out."

"Someone," Lynn said, "might go out on the hull with a cutter."

"In *that*?" Percy asked. That was my thought; my stomach heaved at the idea.

"I could try it," Lynn said.

"You're valuable," Modred said. "The gain would be short term and the risk is out of proportion to the gain."

Like that: Modred's voice never varied . . . like Viv's sums and accounts. I had had another way of putting it all dammed up behind my teeth. But the crew wasn't my business, any more than it was Viv's.

"What are you going to do?" Viv asked. "What are you doing about this thing? Our lady depends on you to do something."

"Let them be," I said, and Viv looked at me, at me, Elaine, who did my lady's hair and had no authority to talk to Vivien. "If it was your job to run the ship you could tell them what to do, but they've done everything right so far or we'd none of us be alive."

"They left us grappled to this thing. Was *that* right? They *talked* to that thing instead of breaking us loose on the instant. Was that right?"

"Grappling on," Modred said, unstoppable in locating an inaccuracy, "was correct. We would have damaged the hull had we kept drifting."

"And talking to it?"

"Let them be," I said, because that argument had hit them: I saw that it had. "Maybe it was right to do. Wasn't that our lady's to decide, and didn't she?"

"*Griffin*," Viv said. "Griffin decides things. And he wouldn't be deciding them if the crew's incompetency hadn't dropped us into this. We were in the middle of the system.

You can't jump from the middle of the system. And they did it to us, getting us into this."

"We were pulled in," Gawain said. "There wasn't any warning. No evasion possible."

"For *you*. Maybe if you were competent there'd have been another answer."

That was Vivien at her old self again: she did it in the house at Brahmani Dali and sent some of the servants into blank. Now she tried it on the crew. I sat up, shivering inside. "Maybe if Viv's hydroponics don't work out, *she* can go out on the hull," I said. It was cruel. Deliberately. It left me shivering worse than ever, all my psych-sets in disarray. But it shut Viv down. Her face went white. "I think," I said between waves of nausea my psych-sets gave me, "you've done all the right things. So it breaks through. It would do it anyway; and so you've talked to it: would it be different if we hadn't? And so it's got us; would we be better off if we'd slid around over the surface until we made a dozen holes it could get in, and it grappled us anyway?"

They looked at me like so many flowers to the sun. Percy and Gawain and Lynn looked grateful. "No," Modred said neatly, "the situation would be much the same."

Viv could scare them. She could scare anyone. She had my lady's ear . . . at least she had had it when she did the accounts; and she had that reputation. But so did I have Dela's ear. And I would say things if Vivien did. I had that much courage. Dela's temper could *make* the crew make mistakes. She could order them to do things that might endanger all of us. She could order Lynn out on the hull. Or other dangerous things.

"We're supposed to be resting," I said. "It's against orders to be disturbing the crew."

"Oh. Orders," Viv said. "Orders . . . from someone who skulks about stealing. I know who gets tapes they're not supposed to have. Born-man tapes. I suppose you think that gives you license to tell us all how it is."

"They might do you good. *Imagination*, Viv. Not everything comes in sums."

That capped it. I saw the look she gave me. O misery, I thought. We don't hate like born-men, perhaps, but we know about protecting ourselves. And perhaps she couldn't harm

me: her psych-set would stop that. But she would undermine
me at the first chance. I was never good at that kind of poli-
tics. But Viv was.

It didn't help my sleep. I was licensed to have that tape, I
thought; I was justified. My lady *knew*, at least in general,
that I pilfered the library. It was all tacit. But if Vivien made
an issue, got that cut off—

I had something else to be scared of, though I persuaded
myself it was all empty. Bluff and bluster. Viv could not go
at that angle; knew already it would never work.

But she would suggest me for every miserable duty my
lady thought of. She would do that, beyond a doubt.

The hammering started up again, tap, tap, tap, and that
hardly helped my peace of mind either. We quarreled over
blame; and *it* meanwhile just worked away. I rolled my eyes
at the ceiling, shut them with a deliberate effort.

Everyone settled down then, even Vivien, but I reckoned
there was not much sleeping done, but perhaps by Modred,
who lacked nerves as he lacked sex.

I drowsed a little finally, on and off between the hammer-
ings. And eventually Lance came back—quietly, respecting
our supposed sleep, not brightening the lights. He went to his
locker, undressed, went to the bath, and when he had come
back in his robe he lay down on his bed next to me and
stared at the ceiling.

I turned over to face him. He turned his head and looked
at me. The pain was gone. It could not then have gone so
badly; and that hurt, in some vague way, atop everything else.

I got up and came around and sat on the side of his bed.
He gave me his hand and squeezed my fingers, seeming more
at peace with himself than he had been. "I was not," he said,
"what I was, but I was all right. I was all right, Elaine."

Someone else stirred; his eyes went to that. I bent down
and kissed him on the brow, and his eyes came back to me.
His hand pressed mine again, innocent of his difficulties.

"Griffin knows," I warned him. I don't know why it slipped
out then, then of all times, when it could have waited, but
my mind was full of Griffin and dangers and all our troubles,
and it just spilled. He looked up at me with his eyes suddenly
full of shock. And hurt. I shivered, that I had done such a
thing, hurt someone for the second time, and this time in the
haste of the hour.

"They quarreled," I said, walking deeper into it. "Lance, we're supposed to help him . . . you understand . . . with the ship. Lady Dela says so. That we're to help. She's afraid, and there's something going on—" The hammering stopped again. This time the silence oppressed me, and a cold breeze from the vents poured over my skin. I put my hands on Lance's sides, and he put his on my shoulders, for comfort. There was dread in his face now, like a contagion. "Bridges," I said. "Whatever-it-is means to use a Bridge to get to us. All the other ships . . . have tubes going in and out of them. They've seen it . . . the crew . . . when they fined down the pictures on the bridge. That's what that hammering is out there."

He absorbed that a moment, saying nothing.

"Lady Dela's not to know yet," I said. "Griffin doesn't want to frighten her."

Lance nodded slightly. "I understand that." He lay there thinking and staring through me, and what his thoughts were I tried to guess—I reckoned they moved somewhere between what was working at us out there and what small happiness I had destroyed for him.

"What are we going to do about it?" he asked finally.

"We're supposed to be back up on the bridge at 1000. All of us. I think Griffin's got something in mind. I hope so."

"It's after 0800, isn't it?"

I turned around and looked at the clock. It was 0836. "I think I should have gotten everybody breakfast. There's still time."

"I don't want it. Others might."

"Lance, you should. Please, you should."

He stayed quiet a moment, then got up on his elbow. "You go start it, I'll come and help."

I got up and started throwing on my clothes again. There was time, indeed there was time; and it was on my shoulders, to see that everyone was fed. Everyone would think of it soon, and maybe our spirits wanted that, even if our stomachs were not so willing.

It took all kinds of strength to face that thing out there, and in my mind, schedules were part of it, insisting that our world went on.

But I kept thinking all the while I rode the lift down to the galley and especially before Lance came to help me, that it was very lonely down there. The hammering was stopped now; and I was in the outermost shell of the *Maid,* so that the void was out there, just one level under my feet while I was making plates of toast and cups of coffee. I felt like I had when I had first to walk the invisible floor and teach my eyes to see—that maybe our Beast didn't see things at all the way our senses did, and maybe it just looked through us whenever it wanted, part and parcel of the chaos-stuff.

Lance came, patted me on the shoulder and picked up the ready trays to take them where they had to go. "I'll take those topside," I said purposefully, meaning Dela, meaning Griffin; and I took them away from him.

He said nothing to that. Possibly he was grateful. Possibly his mind was somewhere else entirely now, on the ship, and not on Dela; but I doubted that: his psych-set didn't make that likely.

Dela was abed, where I looked to find her. She stirred when I touched her bare shoulder, and poked her head up through a curtain of blonde hair, pushing it back to discover breakfast. "Oh," she said, not sounding displeased. She turned over and plumped the pillows up to take it in bed. "Is everything all right then? It's quiet."

"I think it's given up for a while," I lied, straight-faced and cheerfully. "I'm taking breakfasts round. May I go?"

"Go." She waved a dismissing hand, and I went.

Griffin I found asleep too—all bent over his desk in his quarters, the comp unit still going, the papers strewn under him on the surface. "Sir," I said, tray in hand, not touching him: I was wary of Griffin. "Sir."

He lifted his head then, and saw me; and his eyes looked his want of sleep. I set the tray down for him and uncovered it, uncapped the coffee and gave that into his hands.

"It's stopped," he said.

I nodded. "Yes, sir, off and on. It's been quiet about half an hour so far. It's 0935, sir."

He turned with a frown and dug into the marmalade. I took that for a dismissal on this occasion and started away.

"Have you slept, Elaine?"

I stopped. "Much as I could, sir."

"The others?"

"Much as they could, sir." My heart started pounding for

fear he would ask about Lance or discuss my lady, and I didn't want that. "They'll be eating now. They'll be on the bridge soon."

He nodded and ate his breakfast.

So we came topside at the appointed time, to the bridge. The crew took their posts; Lance and Viv and I stood. The quiet about the hull continued, the longest lapse in hours. And that quiet might mean anything . . . that whatever-it-was had finished out there, that the Bridge was built and we had very little time . . . or that it really had given up. But none of us believed the latter.

1005. Griffin delayed, and we waited patiently, no one saying anything about the delay, because a born-man could do what he liked when he had set the schedule. Viv found herself a place on the cushion by the door, alone, because I wasn't about to sit by her; and Lance stood by me.

"Nothing more has come in," Modred said after checking the records from the night. "Everything's as it was."

Transmissions, he meant. All around us the screens showed the old images, the unrefined images, just the glare and the light, the slow creep of measled red and black shading off to purples and greens.

There were footsteps in the corridor outside. Griffin arrived, and Dela was with him, in her lacy nightclothes, her hair twisted up and pinned the way she would do when I wasn't convenient to do it in its braids.

She looked us all up and down, and looked round the bridge, and Viv and the crew rose from their places and stood respectfully—as if she had just come aboard, as if she had just come here for the first time. As if—I don't know why. Neither, perhaps, did the others, only it was a respect, a kind of tenderness.

She looked around a moment at things I knew she couldn't read, at instruments she didn't know, at screens that showed only bad news, but not the worst. And she kept her hands clasped in front of her, fingers locked, and looked again at all of us. All of us. And Lance: her eyes lingered on him; and then on Gawain. "Griffin has talked to me," she said after a moment. "And he wants to fight this thing, whatever it is. And he wants you to help him. You have to. I see that . . .

that if it tries to get in, someday it's going to. And that
means fighting it. Do you think you can?"

We nodded, all of us. We had no real compunction about
it, at least I didn't, small damage that I could do anything—
because it threatened our lady; and it wasn't its feelings we
were asked to hurt.

"You do that," Dela said, and walked away.

And out the door, past Viv. Very small and sad, and
frightened.

I wanted to run after her; I looked at Griffin instead, because we had our orders, and on Griffin's face too there was
such an expression of pain for our lady—I looked at Lance,
and it was the same. And Gawain and Percy and Lynn. Only
Vivien scowled; and Modred had no expression at all.

Griffin made a move of his hand, walked to the counter
where he could face all of us at once. "Here it is," Griffin
said. "They *are* going to get in. Maybe they'll come in suits
and blow our lifesupport entirely, and rearrange it all, because they need something else. They could be some other ship
who's trying to survive here and doesn't mind killing us. But I
don't think so. The tunnels are general; they're everywhere.
And that points to the wheel itself. The station. Whatever it is
we're attached to. I've talked to Dela about it. There's no gun
aboard; but we're going to have to set up some kind of a defense. If they blow one compartment, we can seal it off, so
we'll just redraw the line of defense. But they're going at it so
slowly . . . I think it's more deliberate than that. They've
done it—to all the ships. And maybe time isn't important to
it. To them. Whatever." He looked from one to the other of
us. "What we can't have is someone panicking and blanking
out at the wrong time. If you don't think you *can* fight, tell
me now. Even if you're not sure."

No one spoke.

"Can you, then?" he asked.

"We're high order," Gawain said, "and we don't tend to
panic, sir. We haven't yet."

"You haven't had to kill anything. You haven't come under attack."

That posed things to think about.

"We can," Lynette said.

Griffin nodded. "You find weapons," he said. "Cutting
torches and anything that could do damage. Knives. If any of

those decorations in the dining hall have sound metal in them—those. Whatever we've got that can keep something a little farther away from us."

So we went, scouring the ship.

. . . but in all the listening eyes
Of these tall knights, that ranged about the throne,
Clear honor shining like the dewy star
Of dawn, and faith in their great King, with pure
Affection, and the light of victory,
And glory gain'd, and evermore to gain.

X

It was one of those *long* days. We scoured about the ship
in paranoid fancy, cataloguing this and that item that might
be sufficiently deadly.

Of course, the galley. That place proved full of horrors.

And the machine shop, I reckoned: the crew spent a long
time down there making lists.

And of course the weapons in the dining hall and Dela's
rooms. They were real. And it was time to take them down.

That was Viv and I. I stood on the chairs and unscrewed
brackets and braces while Viv criticized the operation and re-
ceived the spears and the swords below. And my lady sat
abed, so that I earnestly tried to muffle any rattle of metal
against the woodwork, moving very slowly when I would turn
and hand a piece to Viv, who was likewise quiet setting it
down.

I thought about the banners, whether we should have them;
the great red and blue and gold lion; the bright yellow one
with green moons; the blue one with the white tree; and all
the others. And I thought of the stories, and it seemed important, if we had the one we should have the other—at least the
lion, that was so gaudy brave.

107

"That's not part of it," Vivien said when I attacked the braces.

"Oh, but it is," I said. I knew. And Viv stood there scowling. I handed it toward her.

"It's *stupid*. It doesn't do anything."

"Just take it."

"I'm not under your orders."

"Quiet."

"*Who*'s quiet? Put that back and get down off the chair."

"I'm not going to put it back. At least get out of my way so I can get down."

"Elaine?"

Dela's voice. "See?" I said. It was stupid, the whole business. I turned the cumbersome standard with its pole so that I could gather the banner to me, and stepped down from the chair, having almost to step on Viv. We can be petty. That too. And Viv was. Too good for menial work. It was me my lady called and we don't call out loud like born-men, shouting from place to place. I hurried across to the bedroom door and through, with my silly banner still clutched to me and all the while I expected Viv was right.

"Elaine, what's that you've got?" My lady sat abed among her lace pillows, all cream lace herself, and blue ribbons.

"The lion, lady."

"For what?" my lady asked.

"I thought it should make us braver."

A moment Dela looked at all of me, my silly notions, my other self, *that* Elaine. Her eyes went strange and gentle all at once. "Oh my Elaine," she said. "Oh child—"

No one had ever called me that. It was only in the tapes. "Lady," I said very small. "Shall I put it back?"

"No. No." Dela flung off the covers, a flurry of lace and ribbons, and crossed the floor; I stepped aside, and she went through into the sitting room, where we had made a heap of the weapons, where Viv stood. And she bent down all in her nightthings and gathered up the prettiest of the swords. "Where are these to go?" She was crying, our lady, just a discreet tremor of the lips. I just stood there a heartbeat still holding the lion in my arms.

"Out to the dining hall," I said. "Master Griffin said we should bring all the things there because it was a big place and central so—"

—so it wouldn't get to our weapons store when it got in; that was the way Griffin put it. But I bit that back.

"Let's go, then," said Dela.

"Lady," Vivien said, shocked. But Dela nodded toward the door.

"Now," Dela said, taking up another of the swords and another, and leaving Vivien to gather up the heavy things. Me, I had the lion banner, and that was an armful. Dela headed out the door and I followed my lace-and-ribboned lady—not without a look back at Vivien, who was sulking and loading her arms with spears and swords.

So we came into the dining hall turned armory, and I unfurled the lion and set him conspicuously in the center of the wall, to preside over all our preparations. There was kitchen cutlery and there were pipes and hammers and cutters, and the makings of more terrible things, in separate containers—

"What are those?" Dela asked.

I had no wish to answer, but I was asked. "Chemicals. Gawain says we can put them in pipes and they'll blow up."

Dela's face went strange. "With us in here?"

"I think they mean to carry them down to the bow and not make them up till then. They're working down there—Master Griffin and the others. They don't mean they should get through at all."

"What else is there to do?"

I thought then that she *wanted* something. I understood that. I wanted to work myself, to work until there was no time to think about what was going on outside. From time to time the hammering stopped out there and then started again. And I dreaded the time that it would stop for good, announcing that they/it/our Beast might be ready for us. "There's all of that to carry and more lists to make; we're supposed to know where all the weapons are; and food to make and to store in here and the refrigeration to set up—in the case," I finished lamely, "we should lose the lower deck."

Viv had arrived, struggling with her load, and dumped it all. "Careful," my lady said sharply, and Viv's head came up—all bland, our Viv, but that was the face she gave my lady.

"And they're welding down below," I finished. "They're cutting panels and welding them in, so if they think they've gotten through the hull, they've only got as much to go again."

"We should all help," my lady concluded. "All."

"I have my work upstairs," Viv said; she could get away with that often enough, could Viv. I have my books; I have accounts to do; and Go do that, my lady would say.

Not now. "You can help at this," my lady said, very sharp and frowning. "Make yourself useful. You're not indispensable up there."

Oh, that stung. "Yes, lady," Vivien said, and lowered her head.

"I'll get the rest of the weapons," I offered.

"No," my lady said, "Vivien can start with that. Get the galley things in order."

"Yes," I said. It was no prize, that duty, but it was the one I well understood.

"I'll be down to help," my lady said.

"Yes, lady," I murmured, astonished at the thought, and thinking that I would have one more duty to care for, which was Dela herself, who really wanted to be comforted. I left, passed Vivien on my way out the door and hurried on to the lift, wiping my hands on my coveralls.

I took the lift down. The ship resounded down there not alone with the crashes and thumps of the thing outside, but with the sounds of Griffin and the others working, trying to put a brace between ourselves and the outside.

The galley was close enough to hear that, constantly, and it reminded me like a pulsebeat how the time was slipping away, and how we had so little time and they had all the time that ever might be in this dreadful place.

Other ships must have fought back. Nothing we had seen gave us any true hope. But I went about the galley reckoning how we could store water—we have to have water in containers, Griffin had said, because they might find a way to cut us off from the tanks. And we have to have the oxygen up there; the tanks and the suits. The whole ship had to be re-planned. We had to think like those would think who wanted to kill us; and I was never trained for such things—except in my dreams. I set my mind to devious things, and reckoned that we must take all the knives and dangerous things out; and my lady's good silver too, because they should not have that, nor the crystal. And all our medical supplies must come up.

And the portable refrigeration. That came first. We had it in the pantry, and I got down with a pliers I had from upstairs, and on my hands and knees I worked the bottom transit braces loose. Then I climbed up on the counter and attacked the upper braces.

So Dela found me, sweating and panting and having barked my fingers more than once—but I had gotten it free. "Elaine, call Percy," she said: it was always Percy we called for things like this.

"Lady, Percy's helping Master Griffin. They all are. I can manage."

My lady looked at it uncertainly; but when I pushed from the back she wrestled it from the front, and the two of us got it out. I looked at her after, Dela panting with maybe the first work but sport she had ever done; her eyes were bright and her face flushed. "To the lift?" she asked.

I nodded, dazed. And she set her hands to it, so there was nothing to do but push . . . through the galley and over the rough spot of the seal track, down the corridor toward the lift. And all the while that frenetic banging away toward the bow of the ship, toward which Dela turned her head distractedly now and again as we pushed the unit up to the lift door. But she said nothing of it.

We took it up; we wrestled it down the corridors and over section seal tracks and into the dining hall pantry where we decided was the best place to put it. "We have to brace it again," I said. It was too heavy to have rolling about if the ship should shift or the like. So my lady and I contrived to get it hooked up and then to get it fastened into a pair of bottom braces.

And we sat there in the floor, my lady and I, and looked at each other. She reached over and put a hand behind my neck, hugged me with a strange fervor; but I understood: it was good to work, to do something together when it was so easy to feel alone in that dinning against our hull, and in our smallness against *that* outside.

We got up then, because there was the food to fetch up, and the water tanks. It was down again in the lift, and filling carts with frozen food and taking it up again; and hunting the tanks out of storage.

"The good wine," Dela said. "We should save that."

"And the coffee," I said. My knees were shaking with all this pushing and climbing and carrying. I wiped my face and felt grit. "My lady, I think everyone might like to have something to eat."

She thought about that and nodded. "Do that," she said. "We can take something to Griffin."

"I can do that," I said, thinking how grim it was forward, where they were building our defenses.

But Dela was determined. So I made up as many lunches as I knew there were workers forward, which was everyone but Vivien; and we took the trays into that territory of welding stench and hammering, where the crew and Lance worked with Griffin.

They stopped their work, where the hallway had suddenly shortened itself in a new welded bulkhead improvised of a section seal and some braces. They were scorched and hot—the temperature here was far too high for comfort. And eyes widened at the sight of Dela: people stood up from their work in shock, Griffin not least of them, and took the trays Dela brought, and looked at her in a way that showed he was sad and pleased at once.

"We've got a lot of the upstairs work done," Dela said, "Elaine and I."

Griffin kissed her: we had washed, my lady and I, and were more palatable than they—a tender gesture, and then the They across the division boomed out with a great hammering that made us all flinch, even Griffin. "No need for you to stay here," Griffin said.

But my lady took a tray and sat right down on the floor, and I did; so all the rest settled with theirs. I saw the crew dart furtive disturbed glances Dela's way: she shook their world, and even Modred, who was too close-clipped to be disheveled ever, still looked disarranged, sweating as we all began to, and with exhaustion making lines about his eyes. Percy had hurt his hand, an ugly burn; and Gawain had his beautiful hair tied back in a halfhearted braid, and some of it flying about his face; and Lynette, close-clipped as Modred, had her freckled face drowned in sweat that gathered at the tip of her nose and in the channels of her eyes. Lance—Lance looked so tired, never lifting his eyes, but eating his sandwich and drinking with hardly a glance at us . . . or at Dela sitting next to Griffin.

"We're going to make braces for sealing more than one point in the ship," Griffin said. "Lower deck; and the mid-decks. If they get to top—they've got everything. Only the topmost deck and the hydroponics . . . we draw our final defense around that, if it has to be."

"One of us might still go out there," Lynette said. "Might still try to see what they're up to."

"No," Griffin said.

"We could try." Lance lifted his head for the first time. "Lady Dela, if one of us went out and tried to get into the thing—"

"No," Dela said, with finality.

"They could learn us," Griffin said. "It's not a good idea. With one of us in their hands. . . . No. We can't afford that. But we'll see; it's possible—they have rescue in mind. One can hope that."

It was a thought to cherish. But I remembered that voice on the com, and how little it was like us. And the ships, pierced by the tubes like veins, bleeding light through their wounds.

Perhaps everyone else thought of that. The surmise generated no cheer at all, not even from my lady.

And time, as time did in this place, weighed heavy on us, so that it felt as if we had been all day at work instead of only half. Maybe it was the battering at our hull, that went on and on; and maybe it was a slow ebbing of the hope that we tricked ourselves with, that wrung so much struggle out of us, when a little thought on the scale of things was sufficient to persuade us we were hopeless.

I longed for the plains of my dreams, I did, and the horns blowing and the beautiful colors and the fine brave horses Brahman had never seen. But here we sat dirty and scorched with the welding heat and with the hammering battering at our minds; and never room or chance for a good run at our Beast. I looked up at Lance, wondering if *he* longed the same. I saw his eyes lifted that once, but it was a furtive glance toward Dela with all that pain on his face that might have been exhaustion. Might have been. Was not.

That was never changed.

"We'd better get to work," Griffin said.

So we gathered up our used trays and weary bones; and we carried them back to the galley, Dela and I, while the others set themselves to their business.

There was food to be carried up; and we filled tanks and ran them up; trip after trip in the lift, until my lady was staggering with the loads. And we broke a bottle of the wine, glass all over the corridor, which I hastened to mop up, picking up all the glass. It was like blood spilled there, everywhere, running along the channels of the decking: I thought of that, with our clothes stained with it from the spatter, and the hammering that never stopped. My lady looked distracted at the sight—so, so small a thing threatened her composure, when larger things had not. We were tired, both of us.

"Where's Vivien?" Dela wondered sharply, with that tone in her voice that boded ill for the subject. "Where's Vivien all this time?"

"Probably at inventory," I offered, not really thinking so. "I'll go find her."

"I will," my lady said, with that look in her eye.

I kept working. That was safest.

And it was not until my next trip topside that I found Viv, who was busy storing items in the freezer. Immaculate Vivian. No hair out of place. At least she was working.

I added my own cart to the lot and began to help. "Did my lady go to rest?" I asked: it was evident Dela had found her—very plain in Viv's sullen enthusiasm for work. But Dela was nowhere about the dining hall.

"She went to take a bath," Viv said, all brittle. "You might, you know."

"I'm sure you haven't worked up a sweat."

Viv rounded on me, with such a look in her eyes, on her elegant oval face, that I had never seen. *"You,"* she said. Just *you,* as if that were all the fault. Her lips trembled; her eyes brimmed.

"Viv," I said, contrite, and reached out a hand: I was greatly shaken, not having seen that coming.

She struck my hand down and turned her face away, went on about her work. My lady must have been very hard with Viv. And now and again while we worked she would wipe fiercely at her eyes.

"Viv, I'm sorry."

"Oh, was it *your* doing?" She looked at me again. It would

have made me laugh, because I had never seen Viv's face like that, with the mascara smeared like soot. But I was far from laughter. It was like seeing wreckage. Viv started to cry; and I put my arms about her, just held on to her until she had gotten her breath and shoved me back.

That was all right. Viv was afraid as well as mad and tired. I knew what that felt like. "It's all stupid," she said. "It's none of it going to work."

Viv indeed had a mind.

"Griffin says they might be trying a rescue after all," I offered.

"They're not," Vivien judged, and turned her shoulder to me.

I emptied the cart and took it down for another load.

So my lady had had her fling at work and bravely at that, and now she had exhausted herself enough to rest; but I had things yet to do. And Griffin and those with him—they were only now bringing their equipment up the corridor to lift it to middecks, clatter and bang.

It was lonely down there after they had gone; I worked there by myself, loaded up two carts with the last that we had to bring up.

What if it should break through of a sudden, I thought. What if it should be now? I pushed my carts into the lift and rode it up into safer levels, the hammering distant up here and easier to forget.

So we fought, with our wits and our small resources; and the deadliest things we had found in all the ship were the welders that Griffin used to fortify our poor shattered bow.

Viv was not talkative. It was not a good day for her, not in any sense. She sulked about the things we had to do together, and her hands shook when the pounding from belowdecks would get loud. She complained of headache; doubtless that was true. I thought that I might have one if I slowed down and let it have its way.

But Dela came out of her retreat again, bathed and fresh, and helped us, which I think scandalized Viv, and which Viv blamed me for. All the same the working comforted Dela, and she smiled sometimes, braver than we when she had a task under her hands: only sometime the façade cracked and I could see how nervous she was, how her eyes would dart to small sounds. Viv hardly knew how to react to this: I think it

was the first time my lady had ever gotten to watch Viv work,
which was, excepting Viv's trained functions, dilatory and involved much motion over little result. And Viv was trying to
reform this tendency under that witness, but habit was strong.
It would have been funny except that poor Viv was so distracted and so unhinged I remembered the tears.

We knew, when we were finished, how much of everything
we had, and we had taken a great deal of it into storage on
main level, including bedding enough for us all if we had to
sleep here; and we had filled the huge tanks for Vivien's
domain topside. Vats and pipes everywhere up there; but
there was a lot of water involved, and we felt the more se-
cure for that. That was another thing that gnawed at Viv,
because my lady insisted on Viv telling her what it all did
while I was there to hear it—because, my lady said, something might happen to one of us. Poor Viv. That was not the
thing she wanted to think about.

But came the time that all of us had run out of strength,
and Griffin's party came up to the dining hall, all dirty as
they were, to the dinner we fixed on the last of our
strength—even Viv's. And Lynn looked ready to fall over on
the table, sitting there stirring her soup about without the
strength to get it to her mouth, and Modred was as down as I
had ever seen him, not mentioning the others, who had burns
and cuts from the metal and who looked as if a dinner at
table was only further torment. They would probably rather a
sandwich in solitude, and maybe not that. Griffin was drawn
as the rest of them . . . as worn, as miserable; but he
smiled for Dela, and made a joke about frustrating our attackers.

Then there was a signal from the bridge, which meant that
something had happened, and we staggered away from our
supper, all of us.

It knew, I thought, it *knew* that we were trying to rest: *our*
hammering had stopped, and maybe it picked up that silence
inside. So we stood shivering on the bridge, under the images
of the dead ships and the bleeding space outside, and listened
to that nonsensical sound that rumbled and roared like a
force of nature. Even Dela was there to hear, and Viv—Viv
just blanked, frozen in the center of the room.

"Respond?" Modred asked.

"No," Griffin said.

"I might point out—"

"No," Griffin said. "No more reaction to it. They know too much about us already, I'm afraid."

Modred cast a look toward my lady, not real defiance; but there was that manner to it. "I might point out we have defenses. But they're worth nothing in the long term. We should talk while we have something to talk with. I have a program—"

"No," Dela said, ending that. Modred only looked tired, and turned back to the board.

"Leave it," Griffin said. "All of you—go below and sleep. All of us can use it. Hear?"

We heard. Modred shut down; Gawain left his place, and Lynn and Percy did. Myself, I wanted nothing more than to go down to my own bed and rest. I saw my lady go off arm in arm with Griffin; and remembered the dishes with an ache in my bones and a wish to leave them and go curl up somewhere.

No Viv. Percy had gotten her by the arm and they were on their way out the door. Only Lance stayed, looking like death and all but undone.

"Can't come," I said. "I've got the dishes."

"I'll help," he said. We worked like that, Lance and I, both of us staff and responsible for our born-man and for the things not in anyone else's province. So he came with me. I don't know which of us was more tired, but I reckoned it was Lance: his poor hands were burned and the china rattled in them—I reckoned that water would hurt on the burns so I did all the washing.

And after that, we went to see to our born-men, who were together: nothing to do there. Dela and Griffin were locked in each other's arms and fast asleep. I looked back at Lance who had come closer to the door, made a sign for quiet—but he only stood there, and a great sadness was on his face.

I dimmed the lights they had forgotten or not cared about. "Come on," I whispered, and took him by the arm, walked with him outside and closed the door.

"Go on down," he said. "I'll stay hereabouts."

"Lance, you shouldn't. You're not supposed to."

"He's good to me—you know that? He knows, like you said. And he loves her. And all of today—he never had any spite. Nothing of the kind. And he might have. Anyone else would have. But he treats me no different for it."

"He's all right," I said finally. "Better than any of the others."

"Not like any of the others," Lance said. He shook his head, walked away with his head bowed—the way Griffin had walked away that night, as sad. Not like the others. Not someone Dela would tire of. Not someone to put aside. And kind. Maybe he wished for Robert back. But Lance was in the trap. He had so little selfishness himself—he opened to generosity. He was made that way.

"Lance." I caught up with him, took his arm. "Lance—I don't want to be alone." I said it, because he had too much pride. He let me take his hand. "Come downstairs," I asked him.

He yielded, never saying anything, but he walked with me to the lift, and I was all but shaking with relief, for pulling him out of that. We should have a little comfort, we two, a night lying close, among our friends.

We came in ever so quietly, Lance and I, into the mostly dark sleeping quarters . . . stood there a moment for our eyes to adjust, not making any noise. Everyone was on the couches, and a tape was running; the screen flickered. I was sorry that we had missed the start, because it was maybe the best thing to do with the night, to be sure of quiet dreams. We could still hear the hammering.

We might slip in on the dream, I thought: when my eyes had adjusted enough that I reckoned not to bump into anything, I crossed the room and looked up at the screen to know what sort it was.

And then my heart froze in me, and I flew back across the room to my locker, and Lance's. I felt there, on the shelf, but the tape was gone; was in the machine; running, and they were locked into it—*all* of them.

Maybe my face showed my terror. Lance had seen; he looked only half disturbed until he looked at me, and reached out his hand for mine. "Viv," I said, reckoning who would have stolen. "O Lance, we're ruined, we're lost, they shouldn't—"

"We can't stop it," he said, half a whisper. "We daren't stop it halfway—not that one. They'd never sort it out."

"It's my fault," I mourned. "Mine." But he put his arms

about me and held, which was comfort so thorough I had no good sense left and held to him, which was all I wanted.

"We might use it too," he said. "If it's beyond stopping. I want it, Elaine."

So did I, for twisted, desperate reasons—even if I lost him again. So we joined them, helpless in the dream that had gotten loose on the ship, that filled the *Maid* and told us what we might have been.

But for some of us it was cruel.

Then that same day there past into the hall
A damsel of high lineage, and a brow
May-blossom, and a cheek of apple-blossom,
Hawk-eyes; and lightly was her slender nose
Tip-tilted like the petal of a flower;
She into hall past with her page and cried,
". . . Why sit ye there?
Rest I would not, Sir King, an I were king,
Till ev'n the lonest hold were all as free
From cursed bloodshed, as thine altar-cloth
From that best blood it is a sin to spill.
My name? . . .
Lynette my name.

XI

It was a good way to have passed that aching night—if it had been any other tape. We were free for a time; we knew nothing about the terrible place where we were.

I loved and lost again. But I knew the terms. And there was Lance with me, who had learned the tape under his own terms, and who had made his peace with what he was. He was trapped, the same as I was. And not afraid anymore. His world made sense to him, like mine to me.

But when we woke, with the hammering still going on the same as before—when we stirred about with the light slowly brightening to tell us it was another morning in this place—it was hard to look at one another. Everyone—crew and staff—moved about dressing, and no one looked anyone else in the eye.

That was what it did to us.

I went over and took the tape myself, and no one said anything; I stored it in my locker again. But they all knew where, and I reckoned so long as we lasted in this place, they would not let it alone. Could not let it alone. Lance came and laid his hand on mine on the locker door, and pressed my fingers. He was afraid too, I thought. Of the others. Of what now we knew we were.

Only there was Percy, who came to us, his face all distressed. Who just came, and stopped and stared. Gentle Percivale.

"It's a tape," I said out loud, so they all could hear. "It's an old story, an amusement. Lady Dela owns it and let me borrow it. You have to understand."

But there was no easy understanding. Not for that.

"Viv said—" Percivale began, and dropped it.

Vivien. I looked her way; and Vivien met my eyes by accident. She was just putting her jacket on; and her head came up. It was not a good look, that. She turned away and began sweeping her hair back, to put it up again in its usual immaculate order.

"We had better get to the bridge," Gawain said then quietly, "and see how the night went." He started to the door, looked back. Percivale had joined him. And Lynn. "Modred?"

Everyone looked. Modred had been sitting on the couch getting his boots on—and still sat there, inward as ever. And when Gawain called him he got up and went for the door, as silent, as quiet as ever.

But we got up afraid of him, as we had never been. And it was wrong. I felt it wrong. I intercepted him on his way, took his arm.

"It's amusement," I said. But Modred had always been innocent of understandings—without sex, without nerves. "It's a thing that happened a long time ago, if it ever happened."

His dark eyes fixed on mine, and I saw something in the depth of them . . . I couldn't tell what. It might have been pain; or just analysis—something that for a moment quickened him. But he had nothing to say. *Our* Modred could make jokes, the lift of a shoulder, the rhythm of his moves; but this morning he was—quiet. Without this language. He used the quieter story tapes; mostly I suspect they bored him, and the more violent ones were outside his understanding.

But when one is tired, when one's defenses are down to begin with—

"Yes," Modred said, agreeing with me, the way we agree with born-men, to make peace and smooth things over. And he went away with the others.

"Vivien," I said, turning around. "Vivien, you've done this."

She went on pinning up her hair.

"Let be," Lance said, taking me by the shoulders.

She was dangerous, I thought to myself, and she ran all our lifesupport up there; and our future food supply; all the technical things in the loft.

But maybe—I tried to persuade myself—that was what we were all doing this morning: maybe we had all learned to look at each other askew; and we were cursed to know how others saw us.

"Modred," I mourned. "O Modred."

"It should never have happened," Lance said. "It was my fault, not yours."

"How do we prepare against a thief?" I asked, meaning Viv. But Viv had finished her dressing and swept past us without a look.

"My fault," Lance repeated doggedly.

"They'll sort it out," I insisted, turning round to look at him. "You did. I have."

"I'm not so sure," he said, "of either of us."

"You know better than that."

"I don't." He put his hands in his pockets. "Aren't we—whatever tapes they put in?"

I had no answer for that. It was too much like what I feared.

"Elaine," he said sadly. Touched my face as he would have touched Dela's. "Elaine."

And he walked away too.

My fault, I echoed in myself. When they all had gone away, I knew who was to blame, who had been selfish enough to bring that tape where it never should have been.

"What's wrong?" Dela asked at the breakfast table, and sent my heart plunging. We sat, all of us silent: had sat that way. "Is something wrong no one's saying?"

"We're tired," Griffin said, and patted her hand atop the

table. "All of us." He laughed desperately. "What else *could* be wrong?"

It got a laugh from Dela. And a silence then, because some of us had humor enough to have laughed with her if we had had the heart.

O my lady, I wanted to say, flinging the truth out, we've heard what we never should; I stole what I never ought; we know what we *are* . . . and that was the terror of it, that we were and were not, locked together in this place apart from what was real.

"Elaine?" she asked, and touched my face, lifted my chin so that I had to look her in the eyes. "Elaine, don't be frightened."

"No," I said. It did her good perhaps, to comfort *us.* The lion banner looked down on us where we sat at breakfast at the long table among all the deadly things we had gathered. I heard the trumpets blowing when my lady looked at us like that. But louder was the hammering that had never ceased.

Dela smiled at me, a grin broad as she wore for new lovers. But there was only Griffin. It was the banner; it was her fancy moving about her. She smiled at me because I understood her fancy, if Griffin did not— She had her courage back. She had found her footing in this strange place, and there was a look in her eyes that challenge set there.

"I wish there were more to do," I said.

"There *is* more," Lynette said, suddenly from down the table. "Let us go outside. Let us breach *them* and see what they are before they come at us. We've got the exterior lock—"

"No," Dela said.

"I've been up in the observation deck," she said. "I've seen—if you look very hard through the stuff you can *see*—"

"Stay out of there," Griffin said. "It's not healthy."

"Neither," Modred muttered, "is sitting here."

It was insubordinate. I think my heart stopped. There was dead silence.

"What's your idea?" Griffin asked.

"Lynn's got one idea," Modred said. "I have another. First. If you'd listen to me, sir—my lady Dela. We take the assumption that it's not hostile. We feed it information. It's going to stop to analyze what we give it."

"We feed it information and then what?"

"We try the constants. We establish a dialogue."

"And in the end we give away the last secrets we have from it. What we breathe, who we are, whether we have things of value to it—I don't see that at this point. I don't see it at all."

Modred remained very quiet. "Yes, sir," he agreed at last, with that tiniest edge of irony that Modred could put in his flattest voice.

"Modred," Dela said, tight and sharp.

His face never varied. "My lady," he said precisely. And then: "I was working on something I'd like to finish. By your leave."

My heart was racing. I would never have dared. But Modred *had* no nerves. I hoped he had not. He simply got up from his chair. "Gawain," he said, summoning his partner.

"I need Gawain," Griffin said in a level tone, and Gawain stayed. There was apprehension in Gawain's face . . . on all our faces, I think, but Modred's, who simply walked out.

"He's very good," Dela said.

Oh, he was. That was so. That's why they made him that way, nerveless.

"I'd like," Griffin said, "monitoring set up below. Shouldn't be too hard."

"No, sir," Percy said quietly. "Not hard at all."

We dispersed from the table; we cleaned the dishes; we found things that wanted doing, my lady and I; and Vivien. There was the cleaning up of other kinds; there was Vivien's station—

Oh, mostly, mostly after yesterday, after working so hard we ached . . . it was waiting now; and we had so little to do that we found things.

We were scared if we stopped working. And Vivien was in one of her silences, and my lady was being brave; and Lance went down to the gym with Griffin as if there had been nothing uncommon in this dreadful day, the both of them to batter themselves beyond thinking about our Beast.

Might Lynn, I wondered, envying that exhaustion—care for a wrestling round? But no. I had not the nerve to ask. It was not Lynn's style; or mine; and the crew really did find things to do.

Lynn went out in the bubble . . . sat there, hour upon hour, as close to the chaos-stuff as we could get inside the ship. She did things with the lenses there. I took her her lunch up there, trying to keep my back to the view.

"You can see," Lynette advised me softly, "you can see if you want to see."

I knew what she meant. I wasn't about to look.

"I could make it across," she said. Her thin freckled face and close-clipped skull looked strange in the green light from the screens; but out there was red, red, and red. "I could see."

"I know you could," I whispered, hoping only to get out of here without looking at the sights Lynn chose for company. "I'm sure you could. But I know the lady doesn't want to lose you."

"What am I?" Lynn asked. "One of the pilots. And what good is that—here?"

"I think a great deal of good." I rolled up my eyes, staring at the overhead a moment, because something was snaking along out there and I didn't want to see. "O Lynn, what is that out there?"

"A trick of the eyes. A shifting."

"Lynn," I said, because I felt very queasy indeed. "Lynette?"

"*Elaine?*" Of a sudden something was wrong. Lynn rose half out of her chair, pushed me aside; and then—

Take-hold, take-hold, the alarm was sounding: and Modred's voice: "*Brace,* we're going—"

I yelled for very terror. "Let me out of here," I remembered screaming, and flinging myself for the hole that led to the bridge. But: "*No!*" Lynn yelled, and grabbed me in her arms, hugged me to her and I hugged her and the chair and anything else solid my fingers could reach, because we were losing ourselves—

—back again, a blackness; a crawling redness. I held to something that writhed and mewed like the winter winds round Dali peaks, and hissed like breathing, and grew and shrank—

"—another jump," I heard a distant voice like brazen bells.

"Modred?" another called.

"Griffin?" That was my lady, like crystal breaking.

My eyes might be open. I was not sure. Such terrible things could live in one's skull, eyeless and unaided in this place. "We've jumped again," the thing holding me said, the voice like wind.

"Are we free?" I cried. "Are we free?" That was the greatest hope that came to me. But then I got my eyes cleared again and I saw the familiar red chaos crawling with black spiders of spots. And the veins, all purple and green; and the thing to which we were fixed. That was unchanged.

"We're not free." It was Percivale's voice, thin and clear. "It jumped again; but we're not free."

There was a moment of silence all over the ship, while we understood the terms of our captivity. Like all the ships before us.

"O God," Dela's voice moaned. "O dear God."

"We're all right." Griffin's voice, on the edge of fright. "We're all right; we're still intact."

"Situation stable," Modred's cold clear tones rang through the ship. "Nothing changed."

Nothing changed. O Modred. Nothing changed. I clutched the cushion/Lynn's arm so tight my fingers were paralyzed.

"You might have been out there," I said. It was what we had been talking of, a moment/a year ago. "You could have been outside in that."

Lynn said nothing. I felt a tremor, realized the grip she had on me. "We're stable," Lynn echoed. "It must happen many times."

"The hammering's stopped," I whispered. It was so. The silence was awesome. I could hear my heart beating, hear the movement of the blood in my veins. We were so fragile here.

"That's so," Lynn said. She let me go and pushed me back, leaned forward to reach the console. "Modred, I get nothing different on visual."

I managed to get my feet under me while those two exchanged observations. I stared at familiar things and they were normal. And almost I wished for that horrid dislocation back again, that chaos ordinary minds would feel. We were no longer ordinary. We had learned how to live here. For a moment we had been *out* of this place, and that was the horror we felt; that drop into normal space again. And comfort was breaking surface again in Hell.

"We're traveling," I said. Lynn looked at me, bewildered a moment. "We're traveling," I said again. "This place *moves*, goes on moving; we must have reached a star and left again."

"Yes," Lynn said with one of her abstracted frowns. "That's very probable.—Do you copy that, Modred? I think it's likely."

"Yes," Modred agreed. "Considerable speed and age. I think that's very much what we're dealing with. We're a sizable instability. And we grow. I wonder what we might have acquired this time."

"Don't." Dela's voice shivered through the com.

"We're old hands," came Griffin's. A feeble laugh. "We know the rules. Don't we?"

"O dear God," Dela murmured.

Silence then, a long space.

And about us in the bubble, the chaos-stuff swirled and crawled and blotched the same as before.

"Is everyone all right?" Percivale asked then. "Do we hear everyone?"

I heard other voices, my comrades. Lance was there with Griffin; and Gawain. "Elaine's with me," Lynn said. "Vivien?"

Silence.

"She's blanked," I said. "I'm going."

"Vivien," I heard over com, again and again. I felt my way, hand-over-handed my way from the bubble to the ladder and to the bridge . . . across it, through the U where Modred and Percivale were at work. "I'm after Vivien," I said.

"Gawain's on the same track," Percivale said, half rising. "She was at her station when it hit—"

I ran, staggered, breaking rules . . . but Viv was weakest of us, the most frightened. I had to wait on the lift because Gawain had gotten there first; I rode it up to the uppermost corridors, floors/ceilings with dual orientation, dual switches, that crazy place where the *Maid*'s geometries were most alien, where Vivien worked in her solitary makeshift lab. I made the inner doors, and there was Lancelot and there was Gawain before me. They knelt over Viv, who lay on the floor in a tuck, her eyes open, her hair immaculate, her suit impeccable; her hands were clenched before her mouth and her eyes just stared as if they saw something indescribable.

They were afraid to touch her. I was. It was not like blanking, this. It was like the wombs. It was—not; because what Viv saw, she went on seeing, endlessly, like a tape frozen-framed.

"Viv," Lance said, looked at me as if I should have some hope neither of them did. I sank down. I touched her, and all her muscles were hard.

"It's your fault," Gawain said, a strained voice. "It's your fault. That tape of yours—that tape—"

It was Lance he meant. Gawain's face was the color of Viv's. His eyes flickered, jerked, searched for something as if he could not get enough air.

"It was my tape," I said. "Mine. And Viv that stole it. Wasn't it? But it's nonsense. It's not important. It's—"

"Viv is *lost*," Gawain said.

"Lance. Lance, pick her up. I'll find a blanket."

He took Viv's wrist, but there was no relaxing her arms. He lifted her by that limb, got his arms under her, his other arm beneath her knees, and gathered her to him. I scrambled up. "Just get her out of here," Gawain said. "Let's just get her *out*."

"How is she?" That was Percivale, on com. "Is she all right?"

"She's blanked out," I said, looking up at the pickup, above all the eerie tubes and lines and vats and tanks and glare of lights. "We've got her. We're coming down."

And then the hammering started again.

Not where it had been. But close.

Up here. Above.

"Oh no," I said, above the chaos of com throughout the ship. "Oh no."

It was more than here. It was at our side. It was at our bow. We were attacked at all points of the ship.

"Something might have come loose," Lance murmured, standing, holding Viv's rigid body in his arms.

"No," Gawain said, calmly enough. "No. I don't think so. Get her to quarters, Lance. Let's get out of here and seal the door."

. . . Why, Gawain, when he came
With Modred hither in the summertime
Ask'd me to tilt with him, the proven knight.
Modred for want of worthier was the judge.
Then I so shook him in the saddle, he said
"Thou has half prevail'd against me," said so—he—
Tho' Modred biting his thin lips was mute,
For he is always sullen: what care I?

XII

So we came down to main level and got out to take the
downside lift—Gawain and I, and Lance carrying Vivien's
rigid weight. Not a flicker from Viv. I stroked her hair and
talked to her the while, and Gawain talked to her, but there
was nothing.

Only when we had come out into the corridor, lady Dela
was there to meet us, on her feet and about as if we had not
been hurled who-knew-where. "Bring her to my rooms," Dela
said. "I won't have her wake alone down there."

So we brought her to Dela's own apartments, to lay her
down on one of the couches in the sitting room; but:

"The bed," Dela insisted, to our shock. "That's easiest for
her."

Surely, I thought, when Lance had let Vivien down there
amid the satin sheets, surely if there was a place Vivien
would come out of her blank, this was it—in such utmost
luxury, in such renewed favor. I knelt down there at the
bedside and patted Viv's face and chafed her stiff hands.
"Vivien," I said, "Viv, it's Elaine. You're in my lady's quar-

ters and my lady's asking after you. You're in her own bed and it's safe, you understand me?"

I doubted that anything reached her. Her eyes kept staring, and that was not good. They would be damaged. I closed them, as if she were dead. In a moment more they opened again.

"Vivien," I said, "you're in Dela's bedroom."

A blink. I got that much out of her, which was much, considering—but nothing more. Outside, from many points of the ship now, I could hear the hammering.

And Vivien had chosen her refuge from it.

I got up from my knees and looked back toward the door into the sitting room, where a door had opened. Griffin had come in; I heard his voice; and Gawain had gone out there. Lance waited for me, and I went with him to join the others—my lady, and Griffin.

"She won't respond," I said very quietly when my lady looked to me for a report, "but her reflexes are back. —It takes time, sometimes."

"I don't understand you," Dela said in distress. *Us*, she meant, compared to born-men. "Why do you *do* that?"

"We aren't supposed to—" I started to say, and the words locked up in my throat the way things would that weren't supposed to be talked about. —We aren't supposed to do things for ourselves, I wanted to say; and blanking's all that's left. She had wanted to do something, Vivien had, but she was made, not born, so she had no way out. Alone. Viv was always alone, even with us.

"Don't any of the rest of you do that," Dela said. "You hear me? Don't you do that."

"No, lady," Lance said with such absolute assurance it seemed to touch both our born-men, while all about us the hammering continued.

On all sides of us now. So all the preparations we had made, every defense Griffin had planned—all of that was hopeless now.

"Call the others to the dining hall," Griffin said. "I want to talk to them."

"Yes, sir," Gawain said, and went.

So Griffin thought that there was reassurance to give us. O born-man, I thought, we aren't like Vivien. We'll go on working now we know the rules, because we know we have work to do for you. You don't have to reach so far to find us hope.

But seeing Vivien cave in as she had done, Griffin believed he had to come up with something for the rest of us. He looked so distressed himself that it touched me to the heart. It was Dela that went to him and held his hand. And Lance just stood there.

"Ah!"

Vivien's voice. A terrible sound, a shriek.

I spun about and flew into the bedroom. There was Vivien wide awake and sitting up as if from some nightmare, the covers clutched to her breast and that same stark horror in her eyes, but waking now.

"It's all right," I lied to her fervently, coming through the door. I ran to her and caught her hands which held the sheets and I shook at her. "Viv, come out of it. You're in Dela's room, you're safe. It can't come here."

"Can't it?" Her teeth chattered. Her hair was mussed, trailing about her face. She gave a wrench to get away from me and I let go. Then she looked beyond me at the others who had come in. I looked around. My lady was there, foremost, and Griffin and Lance. "It's coming through up there," Vivien said. "Right into the lifesupport."

"Maybe we could move the equipment down," Dela said.

Griffin said nothing. Nor did Lance or I, probably all thinking the same.

"It's making those things all around us," Vivien said. "Until it has its tendrils into us and we're done. Nothing we do is working."

"We lose the tanks if it gets in there," Griffin said.

"And then we lose everything," Dela said. "We have to move the lab."

"No," Griffin said. "Come on. Let's go talk to the others."

He took Dela with him. I delayed, with Lance, to see to Vivien, who sat amid the bed with her head fallen into her hands. She swept her hair back, then, adjusted pins, beginning to fuss over herself, which was one of her profoundest reflexes. She could be dying, I thought, and still she would do that. For a moment I felt deeply sorry for Viv.

"Shut up," she said then, when I had said nothing. "Let me alone." She had a way of rewarding sympathy.

"Vivien," Lance said, "get up and come with us."

That was asking for it, giving Viv orders.

"Or we leave you here," I added.

Alone. Vivien got out of bed then, fussed with her suit and brushed at imaginary dirt. Lance held out his hand for her arm, but she pointedly ignored that and walked out ahead of us.

"We're due in the dining hall," I said, being kind, because Viv would have no idea where we were supposed to go and would have had to wait on us otherwise, outside, a damage to her dignity. So she went on ahead of us without a thank you, click, click, click of the trim heels and sway of the elegant posterior and still fussing about her hairpins.

O Viv, I thought with deepest pity, because Lance gave me his strong hand and we walked together; but Viv walked all alone. She was made that way. There was none of us as solitary as Vivien.

Or as narrow. Not even Modred.

We came last into the dining hall, Lance and I and Vivien, but not by much. It was our stronghold, our safe place, the long table under the lion banner, amid the weapons. We could hear the hammering, but more faintly here than elsewhere. We all knew our proper seats and settled into them.

"Have we got a location on the attack?" Griffin was asking.

"Middecks after section," Modred said, "portside. And topside forward. That's main storage and the hydroponics. As well as the action at the bow."

"They're slow about it," Griffin said.

No one said anything to that. We were only glad it was so.

"We look forward," Griffin said then, "to more traveling. To going on and on with this thing. This ship. Whatever it is. But if it travels, it leaves this space from time to time. If we could somehow break loose . . ."

"If you'll pardon me," Modred said, "sir, the crew has been working on that possibility. It won't work."

Griffin's face remained remarkably patient. "I didn't much reckon that it would, but spell it out. Mass?"

"Mass, sir. It's growing with every acquisition, not only the ships, but debris. Mass, and something that just confirmed itself. We're moving. We have an acquired velocity in relation to realspace and there's no means to shed it. This mass has been slingshotted as many times as there are ships gathered out there; if we could hazard an unfounded presumption, and even factoring it conservatively, the acquired velocity would itself increase our mass beyond any reasonable limit. We're a traveling discontinuity, an infinitude, a local disturbance in spacetime. We *are* the disturbance and our own matter is the problem."

I blinked, my hands knotted in my lap under the table, understanding more of what Modred said than I usually did; but Modred was talking down to us. To Griffin.

"If I could reconstruct what happened," Gawain said, "something a long time ago either kicked or pulled the original core object into subspace. And either it never had control or it lost it. So it careens along being attracted by the gravity wells of stars and accelerating all kinds of debris into its grasp. It hasn't got a course. Just velocity. It picks up velocity at the interface and it never gets rid of it. It's no part of our universe any longer."

"We *are* in Hell," Dela murmured, shaking her head.

"Wherever we are," Griffin said, "we have company. And if we can't hope to get out of it, then we have to do something about it. Lynette, you had an idea—to breach the core object itself."

Lynn looked up, eyes aglitter in her thin face.

"I've seen a place," she said, "not so far from the emergency lock starboard. I think we could get into it there."

"And create what kind of difficulty inside the wheel," Griffin asked, "if you breach their lifesupport?"

"We'll rig a Bridge from our own side. Pressure seal. We can do it."

Our eyes went from one face to another—seeing hope, seeing doubt, one and then the other.

"We could save time," Modred said dryly, "by opening our own forward hatch and using theirs."

"We can control matters," Lynn said, "by building our own lock. By having a way round *behind* their position. We could attach to our upper airlock and have a way to attach either to a tube they might build to our upper section or to attach to the wheel itself and have an access *we* control so we don't get trapped."

"And then they move behind *us*, don't they? And we don't know what we're going to meet in weapons. No. It won't work."

"Lynn could be lost out there," Dela said, adding her force to Modred's.

"No, lady," Lynn said. There was that kind of look on Lynn's face that had to be believed while she was saying it. "I can *do* it. Give me the chance. It's all that can stop us being trapped."

"It's worth the try," Griffin said.

"Lady," Modred said.

"I can do it," Lynn said again.

She wanted to so badly: she said it herself, how it hurt to be useless. We all had this compulsion to serve. And Lynn's, I thought, might well be the end of her.

"All right," Dela said.

"Lady—" Modred objected.

"Let her try," Dela said. "Someone has to do something that works."

Modred subsided. His face—I had never seen him so out of countenance—He looked like murder.

"Let's find what we have to use," Griffin said then. But he sat there a moment, as if some of the strength had drained out of him, while our Beast—we knew now for sure it was more than one—battered at the hull on all sides of us.

"We don't really have any choice," Dela said. "We have to do something, and that's all there is left to do, isn't it?"

"That's all there is to do," Griffin agreed.

"Isn't—" Viv asked, breaking the silence she had kept in our councils, "isn't there the shuttle? Couldn't we get off in that?"

Faces turned toward her. "We could use it," Gawain said, "not for that—but to get up against their hull. Without breaching our own."

"And getting back again?" Griffin asked.

"That," Gawain admitted, "not so likely."

"The shuttle might end up anywhere," Lynn said. "It might swing off against the hull somewhere else and we couldn't control it. The only answer has to be a kind of Bridge. That's all that has a chance of working."

"We could get off from the ship," Viv protested.

"No," Lance said patiently, having understood things a long time ago, "we can't. You don't understand, Viv. The shuttle engines are less powerful than the *Maid*'s. And engines only work here, up against the mass."

"Where matter exists at all," Modred added.

Viv simply shut her eyes.

"Don't," Dela said. "Vivien, it's all right."

Vivien didn't understand. She simply didn't want to understand. I think we all knew that much, even Dela, who understood us least of all.

And Vivien opened her eyes again, but she kept her mind sealed, I was sure of that.

"What do you reckon to do?" Griffin asked Lynn. "Do you have it mapped out?"

"There's equipment and parts in storage," Lynn said.

"Let's find it," Griffin said.

So Griffin launched himself—wherever we were now, and whatever had changed since that leap through space we had made. Dela still sat at table after the others had left, and I did, and Vivien did.

"Might I get you something?" I asked Dela.

"No," Dela said hoarsely, her hands locked before her on the table. And so we sat for a while. "He has to do something. That's Griffin's nature. I couldn't let him not do something, could I? But we're in danger of losing Lynn."

"Yes," I said. "I'm afraid we might."

"It's awful, that place out there. It's a terrible way to die."

"Lynn's not that afraid," I said.

Vivien got up from the table and fled, out the door.

"But some of us are," I added.

"Vivien's worthless," Dela said. "Worthless."

"Don't say that. Please don't say that."

"Isn't she?"

"She was very good, with the books. They're just not here, now."

Dela looked up at me, puzzled-seeming. So hard she could be, my lady; but she looked straight at me, not into me, not through me, as sometimes she would. It was as if I had gotten solid enough for her to see. "Do you care?" she asked. "Vivien doesn't care about anyone at all but Vivien."

"She can't," I said, thinking of that tape, *the* tape, and what wounds *that* Vivien had suffered that our own Viv had shared. Like Modred. Like the rest of us. And Lynn. O Lynette, who had to be brave and brash and find a way to *be* that other self if it killed her. My lips trembled. "My lady—" I almost told her. But I couldn't face the rage. "Some of us don't have our sets arranged like that," I said. "Some of us have other priorities."

"I know Vivien's," Dela said. Of course, she knew us all.

"She's Vivien," I said, afraid. "And she would be happy if she weren't."

"That's a strange things to say."

"Like I'm Elaine," I said. "And Lance is Lance."

Dela said nothing at all, not understanding, perhaps, the thing I tried to creep up on, to tell her. She gave me no help. I found the silence heavier and heavier.

"We should *do* something," Dela said. "It would be healthier if we did something." She dropped her head into her hands. I patted her shoulder, hating to see her that way.

"We could go help them," I said. "We can fetch things."

It was unthinkable, that impertinent *we*. But that was the way it had come to be. Dela lifted her head, nodded, got up, and we went to find the others.

We, my lady and I, as if she were one of us, or as if I had been born.

Finding them was another matter. They had disappeared quite thoroughly when we called to them from the lift on one and the other level.

"The holds," Dela said, "if they're going to be hunting supplies."

So we went to the bridge to track them down, because the *Maid* had a great many nooks and dark places where it was difficult to go and no little dangerous.

Especially now.

So we came to the bridge, and found one of them after all, because Modred was at his post, talking to them, running catalogue for them, as it seemed. We walked in, my lady and I, and waited, not to interrupt. After a moment Modred seemed to feel our presence and turned around.

"Where are they?" my lady asked.

"Middecks hold number one section," Modred said. "It's not a good idea," he added then, with never a flicker. "This operation. But no one argues with master Griffin."

"Do what he told you to do," my lady said sharply, and turned and walked out. She had no wish to be told it was hopeless. Neither did I, but I lingered half a breath and looked back at Modred, who had not yet turned back to his post.

"Lynn will die," Modred said, "if she has her own way."

"What can we do?" I asked.

"Be glad it will take them days to be ready."

"And then what?" I asked. "In the meanwhile, what?"

Modred shrugged, looking insouciant. Or dead of feeling. He turned his back on me, which hurt, because I thought us friends, and he might have tried to answer. If there were answers at all.

"Elaine," my lady called, impatient, somewhere down the corridor outside, and I turned and fled after her.

So we found the rest of them, all but Vivien.

They were on middecks, down the corridors from the crew quarters, and bringing parts out of storage by now, out of that section of the *Maid* that was so cold they had to use suits to go retrieve it; the stuff they set out, a big canister, and metal parts, was so cold it drank the warmth out of the air, making us shiver. "We make a Bridge," Griffin explained to us. "We've got the rigging for it if we improvise. We use our own emergency lock on our side, and grip onto whatever surface we choose with a pressure seal, so we can sample their atmosphere before we break through."

Dela said nothing to this. I knew she was not sanguine. But Griffin was so earnest, and so was Lynn, and it was what we had to do.

It was a matter of finding everything and then of carrying it all up the difficult areas of the *Maid*, into places our present orientation made almost inaccessible. We had weight to contend with—and Gawain and Percy got up on jury-rigged ladders in the impossible angles of passages we were never supposed to use in dock as we were, in places where the hammering outside the hull rang fit to drive us mad. We added to it the sound of drills and hammering of our own, making a rig of ropes that would let us lift loads up the slanting deck and get it settled.

We worked, all that day, fit to break our hearts, and most all we had done was just moving the materials into place and making sure that the area just behind the lock was pressure-tight, and that everything they would need was there. Modred never came, nor did Vivien.

It was, I knew, I think more than one of us knew, only another one of Griffin's schemes, that Lynn had been convenient to lend him; and if it had not been this, it would have been another. But it kept us moving; and when we had worked all the day, we went to our quarters exhausted, aching in our arms and elsewhere.

Even Lynn—even she looked hollowed out, as if she had finally gotten the measure of what she had proposed doing, and being tired and full of bruises had beaten the mettle out of her. But she had said no word of giving it up. And no one told Lynn it was hopeless.

Not until we met Vivien.

I suppose that Vivien had been in our quarters most of the day; or in some comfortable hole of her own devising. She was there to meet us when we came in, sitting robed and cross-legged on the couch with one of the study tapes running, a soft murmur that drowned out the tappings from outside. I was glad when I saw her, relieved that she was no longer sick: this was the reflex my psych-set gave me, to be so naive.

But Viv knew where to put a shot.

"You know he'll believe anything now," she said right off, in that low and proper voice of hers. "So now everyone's working to build something to kill the lot of us. It's one project today, and that's not going to work; and what new one tomorrow? It's only worse, and he never knew what he was doing. No more than you do."

We all stood and stared at her, bereft of anything reasonable to say. She got up from the couch like a fire going up, all full of heat and smoke, and we were all disarranged.

"You shouldn't talk like that," I said.

"So she gave him the crew and the ship because it's broken. And the best idea you come up with is going out there with it."

"It's all we *can* do," Lynn said, defending herself.

"Of course, like you didn't move us until it was too late. That was all your idea too. And now you want to make a way for them to get in as if it weren't happening fast enough. You never knew what you were doing."

"Shut up," I said. But Lynn just sat down, elbows on her knees—not staff, Lynette, not prepared against lies that we who dealt with born-men knew how to deal with. The crew was innocent and told the truth. Vivien worked at them in painful ways. "It was all your doing, Viv," I said, "that tape, everything—I know who would have taken it. I know who could be a thief in our quarters. I should stop feeling sorry for you. Everything that ever happened to you, you brought on yourself."

"I took that tape," Percy said in a faint voice, very loud in that quiet. "I did, Elaine. I never expected—*that* . . . I never . . ."

I felt cold all over. I just stood there, wishing that someone would say something, even Viv. Percy's voice trembled into silence, asking answers, and I had never meant to hurt him, not Percy, not any of them.

"We're none of us right," Percy said, looking at me, at Lance. "If we weren't supposed to have it—what is it? And why?"

How do you make sense of a whole life in a why? I shook my head, looked at all the pain I had made, at Lynn who was trying to kill herself, at Gawain who had lost all his cheerfulness and gone sullen; at Vivien who had turned on us; at Percy that I had named a thief, when there was no one more kind and gentle, not even Lance. "The why won't make sense," I said. "But there were people like us a long time ago. Born-men. We can't be what they were. Or maybe never were.'"

"They were ourselves," Gawain said, finding his voice.

"No."

"I never saw myself that way," Gawain said distressedly, far from hearing anything I said. And it was so: that Elaine, myself, me, I—there was no sorting it. She was far more live than I: she loved.

And what did their images—but love, and want, and struggle—things far more live than they? I knew the Lancelot who stood behind me now, who gently put his big hands on my shoulders. And oh, what was Vivien's pettiness to *that* Vivien's malice; or Percy's kindness to *that* Percivale's goodness; or Lynn's bravery to Lynette's? We tried to live, that was what; we caught sight of something brighter and more vivid than ourselves and we wanted that.

Even Vivien—who wanted power, who was made and not born, and who knew nothing about love in either case. She struggled to be more than she was and narrow as she was, it threatened her sanity.

"Oh Viv," I said aloud, pitying.

"Oh Viv," she mimicked me, and turned away, playing the only role she knew how to play, the only one her psych-set and her name fit her for. I stood there trembling.

"Don't listen to her," Lancelot said, his fingers pressing my shoulders.

"She's not to blame," I said. "It's all she can see."

"So what do we do?" Percy asked. "Elaine?"

"We do what we see to do."

"Where's Modred?" Lance asked suddenly.

A silence among us.

"It's not right," I said, "to think about him the way the tape is. Modred's not changed. It can't have affected him, not *him*. We can't all walk off from him. And we can't treat him like that."

"He won't say anything about it," Percy said. "He won't talk."

"He wouldn't," Gawain said.

"He's still working up there," Lynn said, from where she sat, her arms about her thin knees. "He's convinced about his program. He still hopes for that."

"He *wouldn't* do that," Percy said. "Against orders. Not on his own."

Lance's hands were heavy on my shoulders. "Maybe somebody ought to see about him."

"Let him be," Gawain said sharply.

"What's he up to?" Lance asked. And when Gawain stood there staring back at us: "Gawain, what's going on up there?"

Still no answer. Lance let go my shoulders and turned for the door. Gawain started after him and I spun about, "Lance," I cried. "Gawain—"

Gawain overtook him at the door, but there was no stopping Lance when he was in a hurry: he shrugged off Gawain's hand with one thrust of his arm and kept going.

I heard laughter at my back; and not laughter at all, but a very bitter sound, unlike us. I looked back past Percy and Lynn, at Vivien.

"Percy," I pleaded, "Lynn, come on—someone stop them." I headed for the door, knowing everything amiss.

This night a rumor wildly blown about
Came, that Sir Modred had usurp'd the realm
And leagued him with the heathen. . . .

. . . Gawain, surnamed The Courteous, fair and strong,
And after Lancelot, . . . a good knight, but therewithal
Sir Modred's brother, and the child of Lot,
Nor often loyal to his word . . .

XIII

I ran, and was too late for the lift. But Gawain was not: he and Lance were headed topside together, in what state I hated to imagine. Percy and Lynn came running after, and caught me up by the time the lift, empty, had come down again.

"Modred's his partner," Percy said, meaning Gawain's, meaning where loyalties lay. Lynette said nothing; it was like that between them, I thought, while the lift shot us up topside: that Percy and Lynette worked together, were together, that while it was Gawain most often Lynette bedded with—blithe and light Gawain—it was Percivale who worked with her, close, close as ever we could be; like Modred and Gawain.

The door opened and let us out: I ran, but Lynette and Percy ran faster, for the doors where already we heard shouting.

The doors were closed. Locked. Of course, locked. Modred knew his defenses.

"Open up," Lance shouted, and slammed the sealed door

with his fist. But he was staff: he had no right to command
the crew. And Gawain stood there doing nothing to help until
Lynn and Percy came running up ahead of me. "Order him
to open," Lance asked of them, and Lynn: "Modred," she
called. "Modred—" But gently, reasonably.

From inside, no answer.

"Ask him," Percivale asked of Gawain. "He'll listen to
you."

"I doubt it," Gawain said. And so there we stood, the
several of us—oh, it was terrible the look of us, of Lance and
Gawain face to face and glaring at each other—

"It can't happen," I said, tugging at Lance's arm. "O
Lance, go and fetch my lady. He'll listen to *her*. Please.
We're what we always were. We can't have changed; and he
can't. O run, run and tell her. Modred's not well."

He yielded backward to my tugging at him—like tugging
at a rock, it was; but I put myself between the two of
them—him and Gawain. Too proud to back very far: I saw
Lance's eyes. "Percy," I said, "go."

And Percy ran. The lift had worked again, down the corridor. Vivien was there, and I could see she was satisfied . . .
O the malice, the bitter, bitter malice that her makers never
put into her, but the place had given her, and the ruin of all
she was.

"What," she said, "has he shut you out then?"

"Be quiet," Gawain said. "We don't need *you* here."

"Modred," Lynette called, gently, using the com by the
door. "Modred, are you all right in there?"

"He's gone over the brink," Lance said. "Modred, come
out of there. We've sent for my lady. She won't be amused."

Silence from the other side.

"Maybe something *has* happened to him," I said, fearing
more and more. "We aren't right to think the worst of him."

"He hears us," Lance said. "His partner knows what he's
doing. I'd bet on it."

I looked at Gawain, whose beautiful face was flushed with
anger, whose eyes had no little of fear: Lance could beat
him, and there was no doubt of that.

"Wayne," Lynette said, "you covered for him? You *knew?*"

"Should I let you kill yourself and the rest of us?"

Lance reached out very deliberately and took Gawain's

arm, brushed me aside as if I had not been there. "We have orders," Lance said.

And might have said more, but Percy came hurrying back to our relief. "She's coming," Percy said, "my lady and Griffin—" He stopped, transfixed at this sight we made, this laying on of hands that we had never done to each other. But we had nerved ourselves to fight, and had nothing of substance to fight but each other. Lance let Gawain go, further argument abided. And down the hall came Griffin and my lady, in their nightrobes, Griffin with his hair wet from the bath, my lady all a flurry of loose blonde hair and laces and her eyes—oh, my lady's eyes, so full of fright. She knew, *she* knew how wrong we had gone: but Griffin's face was ominous, all threat and anger. He came right through us, punched the com button, slammed his great fist on the door.

"Modred," he said. "Enough of this nonsense. Get this door open."

And more silence. I found myself with my hands clasped before my mouth, like praying. O Modred, I thought, Modred, you can't, you can't defy him. O Lance, O Gawain, do something.

"Modred!" Griffin yelled, another slam of his fist.

And my lady slipped past and leaned up to the com. "Modred. You know my voice."

A delay. "Yes, lady Dela." Like himself, it was, all quiet and untroubled as Pass the salt, please.

"Modred, I want this door open."

"In a moment, my lady."

In a moment. O Modred. Something shivered through me. We had all gotten very still, even Griffin. My lady looked distraught and then gathered herself.

"What are you doing, Modred?"

Silence.

"Modred, what do you think you're doing?"

Silence. A long silence. "That *program* of his—" Griffin said. "That program he wanted to use—"

"Modred," lady Dela said. "I want this door open right now. I want you to shut down what you're doing and come out here. No argument."

A longer silence.

"We'll have to get the cutters," Griffin said.

"Modred. Did you hear that? Are we going to have to do the *Maid* damage on account of you? Open the door."

It opened, so unexpected it jolted all of us—whisk! and he was standing there facing us across the bridge, a black figure against the comp lights and the screens that showed nothing they had not showed before.

"Get him out of there," Griffin said, and Lance and Percy moved in, took Modred's arms—nothing. No countermove. Modred gave way to them and would have let them take him out now, but Griffin barred the way, and the rest of us, and lady Dela.

Griffin put his hand in the middle of Modred's chest and stopped him face to face. "What have you done?" Griffin asked.

"Discover that," Modred said, "sir."

"Modred," Dela said—not angry, not anything but stunned. Modred looked at her then, and even he had to feel something: we're made that way. It had to be pain all the way to the gut, every psych-set torn. But Modred had no nerves. His expression hardly varied. "My lady Dela," he said equably, "I've sent it out, all of it."

"Contacting that thing?"

"It's done."

"And what did you get from it," Griffin asked. "Anything?"

"I was working on that. If you'll let me continue—"

I don't think he even understood it was effrontery.

"Not likely," Griffin said.

"How could you do a thing like this?" Dela asked. "Who gave you leave? Did I?"

"No," Modred said.

"And what have you sent out? *What* have you told it?"

"Mathematics. Chemistry. Our chemistry . . . in symbolic terms."

"Then it knows what we are," Griffin said.

"As well as I could state it."

"Get him out of here," Griffin said. "Lock him somewhere."

"Sir," Lance said. "Gawain knew."

Griffin looked at Gawain, and Gawain's face went white.

"Then we'll be talking to you as well," Griffin said.

"Sir," Gawain breathed and bowed his head.

Griffin looked about at all of us then, and I felt my bones

go cold. "Get him out," Griffin said then and Lance and Percivale took Modred past me without argument from Modred. I stood, close to blanking, knowing what I had done.

"Staff's dismissed," Griffin said. "Go about your business. We'll straighten this mess up. Now. Out. Crew stays."

I fled, down the corridor after Vivien, disheveled as I was. My bones ached, somewhere inside the terror and the confusion: we had worked ourselves until we staggered with exhaustion, and now this—this, that was somewhere at the bottom of it my doing.

I went down and washed and put on clean clothes, because I knew there was no hope of sleep. Our night was over before it had started.

"See," Vivien said, "how organized it all is. No one knows what's afoot." She looked up and about her, where the noise continued, maddening, lifted her hands to her ears as if that could give a moment's relief. "They lost all our chances days ago."

"Shut up," I said, zipping my clean jacket and pulling my hair from the collar. "If you're so efficient, go back to your lab."

Oh. Cruel. Viv turned such a look on me that was hate and terror at once.

"Or do something outside *yourself*, Viv. Be something larger than you are. Think how to protect that lab of yours. Come up with something. Help us, for once."

"Elaine the fair."

"Don't be trapped by it. By the tape. You don't have to be. Oh, Viv—"

"Percy talks about God," she said. Gleaming behind the hate in her eyes was outright terror. " '*He* found God,' our Percy says. And what kind of thing is that for one of us? What's for *me*? You've all gone mad . . . and Percivale's gone and Modred— What of this wouldn't have happened without you? I think it's funny. Oh, it's a fine joke, Elaine."

"Hush, be still."

"What, be still? *Me*, who could work miracles in that stupid tape . . . Let me do one enchantment and I'd be out of here, let me tell you, sweet Elaine."

"Couldn't it be *we*?" I asked. "It's always I, isn't it?" I went for the door. Stopped, hearing uncharacteristic silence at my back.

She might have been upset, I had thought. But there was that terrible anger on her face, a sullenness unlike Modred's nerveless quiet.

"He talks about *God*," she said. "We're all rather above ourselves, aren't we? Like Modred."

She had stopped caring for living. That was the way she had coped with the shocks. I saw that suddenly, and it made me cold. She jumped from attacking Lynn to attacking Modred, to Griffin, to whoever had tried to do anything to change what was. Most of all she had me to blame, when the threat had gotten to the lab and the tape had gotten to her: that was twice she had had her functions shaken apart—and now there was just the tape, and her own defenses.

Percy talking about God and Modred turning on us—and Lance and Gawain at odds. . . .

O God help us, I thought, which was unintended irony. We're all lost in Dela's dream.

And in it we faced our war.

They were busy on the bridge, Percy and Gawain and Lynette and Griffin and my lady Dela—there was nothing I could do there. They were busy trying to figure out what Modred had done on the bridge; but Modred was very good and I doubted they could find it at all if Modred had taken pains to hide it.

And Lance guarded the small room down the corridor which was a small cabin we had used on other voyages, where he had found to put Modred, I reckoned. Lance stood there, against the wall by the door, not moving, and looked tired beyond reckoning. "I can get a chair for you," I offered. "Is there anything I can do?"

"I'm well enough," he said, "but I'd like the chair, thanks."

I brought it, out of Dela's rooms, and set it down for him. He sank into it, with shadows round his eyes, with his big shoulders bowed. There was nothing anywhere to be happy about . . . and still that hammering continued.

I knelt down, took Lance's hand and looked up at him, which was the only way I could have his attention on me. It was focused elsewhere until then—somewhere insubstantial, maybe, on my lady, on our prospects. On what craziness brought him to lay hands on Gawain. I had no idea. His thoughts had grown complex, and they had never been that before. But he saw *me* because he had to, and his fingers tightened a little on my hand, cold and loose in mine until that.

"We've done all we can do," I said. "Lance—it's still all right. He can't have done us that much harm. Let me talk to him, can I? I always could talk to him. I might make sense of him."

"You don't know what might be in his head."

"I know you'll be right outside," I said in all confidence. His eyes flickered—it was a touch of pride, of what his shadow was. He wanted so much—so many things. For him a little praise was much.

"I think," he said, "he got nothing at all to eat or drink yesterday: he might want that."

Break Modred's neck he might; but cruelty was not in Lance. He thought of such things. I nodded.

"I think he might," I said, and got up and went off about that, while Lance kept his watch at the door.

So I came back from the dininghall stores with a sandwich and a cup of coffee, and Lance got up and let me through the door. Just a moment he stayed there, while Modred got up from the bed where he had been sitting, but Lance said nothing, and Modred said nothing, until Lance had closed the door.

"You haven't had anything to eat," I said.

"Thank you."

As quiet as before, as precise and proper, his thin hands clasped before him.

"Modred, why did you do a thing like that?"

He shrugged. "Thank you for the food," he said. I had not set it down. He meant I should leave, that was clear.

"Doesn't it hurt?" I asked. "Haven't you got any nerves at all?"

"If they make the bridge across, they might be right or wrong. But they don't *know*. And it's reckless."

Modred—to talk about recklessness, after what he had done. I set the tray down. "Then why won't you talk to them, tell them what you've done?"

"I don't see that it makes any difference."

"*You* don't see. When did you see everything?"

Another shrug. No one attacked Modred. I stared into that

dark-bearded face that frightened born-men and tried not to think of the tape, of that *other* Modred.

"Modred, *please* talk to them."

"The program isn't locked," he said. "They'll have had no trouble accessing it."

"You could have asked permission."

"I did."

It was so. I knew that he had done that again and again.

"And if I'm wrong," he said, "there's Lynette's way; but if she's wrong—there's nothing left, is there?"

"You might be *right*. And if you are, come back, beg their pardons, talk to them."

He shook his head, walked over matter of factly and investigated the tray I had brought. "Thanks for the food. I hadn't time yesterday."

"Why won't you talk to them?"

He looked up at me. There was a hint of pain, but he looked down again and unwrapped the sandwich, looking only tired.

"Modred."

A second time he looked up at me. "They will never listen—to *me*—even when they should. Reason won't work, will it—not against what a born-man wants to believe. I've seen that before now."

"Do you understand—what it was in that tape Percy found in the locker?"

"Entertainment. A fancy. The logic on which this ship exists."

And the *Maid* was for him—the reason he existed. So it had gotten through to him. There was no reason in it. Modred had not even the nerves to be afraid: he was only trying to think it through and coming out with odd sums. He took a bite of his sandwich, a sip of the coffee. "It was kind of you to come," he said.

"If you could explain to them—"

"I have explained to master Griffin. I don't think he really understands. Or he looks at my face and stops listening." His brow furrowed. "I've exhausted reason. There's nothing else but what I did." A second sip of coffee, and absently he turned his back on me and walked away.

"Modred, look at me. Don't be like that."

He turned back again. "I don't precisely understand what

kind of reasoning it is. Only that I'm not trusted. And that Griffin commands this ship."

"He's a good man."

"But do you think he's *right*?"

That was the logic that divided us . . . We went by other things; and Modred only on his reckonings.

"I'm still following original instructions," Modred said. "To get us out of this. Vivien has the right idea and none of you will listen to her either."

"You said it can't be done."

"I said there was no escaping the mass. I said other things no one heard."

"You mean talking to that thing."

"It's not attractive. It's dangerous. You don't like things like that. I know."

"You left Gawain in trouble on your account."

"Gawain did as Gawain chose to do."

"Then you're not alone. You can't say no one believes in you."

"Or the tape chose for him. He's my . . . brother . . . in the dream. It's a very dangerous thing, to see one's whole existence, from beginning to end, isn't it? I'm Modred. And not to be trusted. Even if I have the right idea."

"If—"

The door opened, abruptly. Born-men do such things, without a by your leave. It was Griffin.

"I'll see you now," Griffin said, "in the dining hall. Now."

And Griffin left, like that, leaving the door open and Lance standing there.

I was afraid suddenly, seeing the look on Modred's face, that was stark frustration—a born-man could do terrible things to us; there were all our psych-sets. There was all of that.

Modred set the tray and cup down, click, mostly untasted, and straightened his shoulders and walked out, past Lance without a look or a word. Lance followed him directly. I hurried after—knowing nothing else to do and nowhere else to go.

So we all came—not alone Lance and I, but all of us on the ship, the rest of them already gathered there, in that hall beneath the embroidered lion. My lady Dela was at the head

of the table along with Griffin, and my place and Lance's and
Modred's were vacant. We went to our places, Lance and I,
having to pass all that long distance down the table—and
Modred took his after a moment, understanding that was
what was wanted of him. Gawain was there, his hands
clenched before him on the table, not looking up. Percy sat
there equally pale, beside Lynette. And Vivien, whose bright
eyes missed nothing.

"We'll have an account, if you please," Dela said,
"Modred."

"Lady, I think you'll have had access by now to the tape I
used. I'm sure Percy can understand it."

"I don't care to go through it all. I want to know why you
did such a thing."

Dela had not learned what had happened to us—my heart
leapt and sank again in guilty relief—no one had told her
about the stolen tape. I should, and had not the courage. And
then I thought what that would do for Modred, how Dela
would never trust him if she knew what he had heard. Or
Lance. Or look at any of us the same.

And Modred as likely might tell her—having no nerves;
and no knowledge of born-men.

"I explained," Modred said, "that there was a chance of
contacting it."

"He—" I said aloud, my heart beating against my ribs,
"Modred told me, lady Dela, that he had it figured—that if
his plan failed, then—then there was Lynn's, wasn't there?
But if Lynn's failed—then—"

"How many of you consulted on this?" Dela asked sharply.
"Gawain? Elaine?"

"I never—" I said. "I—"

But all of a sudden I was having trouble concentrating, because something had stopped, the noise forward stilled, and
that diminished a great deal the noise that had been constant
with us for days.

"I—" I tried to continue, thinking I ought, trying to gather
a denial, to explain, but Griffin held up his hand for quiet.

"It's stopped out there," Griffin said.

"It's—" Dela said.

And then that Sound was back again, our Beast talking to
us over com. It had *heard*. None of us moved for the mo-

ment, and then Modred got out of his seat, and Griffin did, and the rest of us, as Modred headed out of the room.

We knew where he was going.

"Modred!" my lady cried.

But that did no good either.

. . . but she saw,
Wet with the mists and smitten by the lights,
The Dragon of the great Pendragonship
Blaze, making all the night a steam of fire.
And even then he turn'd; and more and more
The moony vapor rolling round the King,
Who seemed the phantom of a Giant in it,
Enwound him fold by fold and made him gray
And grayer, till himself became as mist
Before her, moving ghostlike to his doom.

XIV

Our Beast snarled at us, whispered to us, a low ticking that
rose and assaulted our ears as we came—shaking us with the
power of its voice. Vivien had come: she clung to the doorway with a kind of demented fixation on the sound. She had
become entranced with her destruction, but that noise got to
the bones and put shivers into the flesh, and Viv was right
now close to sanity, in sheer fright. The crew headed for their
places, but Lance laid hands on Modred to stop him.

"Let him go," Griffin said, and Lance looked at Dela, and
did what he was told. I stood by shivering, physically shivering in the horrid sound. But we were better than we had
been, and braver: my lady stood there with her fingers
clenched on the back of Modred's chair and wanted answers
from him—at once, now, immediately.

"We're getting screen transmission," Percy said, and it
came up, a nonsense of dots and static breakup.

"That's an answer," Modred said calmly. He half turned,

looking at my lady at his back, but receiving no instruction, he turned back again.

"What's it saying?" Griffin asked.

Modred ignored the question, busy with a flood of beeps that came through, and Griffin allowed it, because Modred was doing *something*, and Percy was, and then Lynn and Wayne came over from their posts to watch. It was craziness; the bass clicking stopped and became a maddening loud series of pulses. I wrapped my arms about myself, standing there and not understanding any of it. Griffin and Dela didn't understand: that also I came to believe. But they let the crew work with the computer.

"Equipment's not compatible," Modred said finally, the only word he gave us in all that time. "Stand by: we're getting it worked through comp."

"So it can hear us," Dela murmured. She moved back, shaking her head, and Griffin put his arm about her shoulders.

Lance and I and Viv, we just stood there, not understanding anything—until of a sudden lines began to come across one of the screens and it began to build itself downward into a picture. I wasn't sure I wanted to see—whatever it was. "We can clean that up," Gawain said. The crew began to work, and Percy sweated over the computer in greatest concentration, while Modred intervened with small gestures, an indication of this and that, quiet words. And then Modred reached for another control. Lynn reached out instantly and checked his hand from that. "No," Lynn said.

"My lady." Modred half turned in his seat. "We have to transmit and give it something back to keep its interest. This is going to take us time."

"Give it—what?" Griffin asked.

"The same thing as before," Modred said. "Repeating it. Giving it the notion we're still working."

"All right," Dela said quietly, and Lynette took her hand away, so whatever Modred wanted to send went out.

It went on a long while, this consultation, this meddling with the computer, and sometimes the lines on the screen grew clearer, and sometimes more confused. My knees ached, and my back and shoulders, so that finally I went over to that bench near the door where Vivien had sat down. After a moment more Lance came and took the place by me, silent company, image of other terrible nights trying to cope with this place.

But my heart was tired of beating overtime, and my limbs were all out of shivers. Terror had acquired a kind of mundanity, had become an atmosphere, a medium in which we just went on functioning, and did what we were supposed to do until somehow our Death would get to us. I reckoned that tired as I was it might not even hurt much. Maybe Vivien reckoned that way, sitting by me with her hands clasped in her lap—not blanked at all, but following this; and maybe Lance felt the same—who had Dela and Griffin in front of him, their arms about each other. Only the crew went on driving themselves because they had something left to do.

Our born-men—they had no least idea, I reckoned, what made sense to do, but they stood there, while the voice of our Beast rumbled away over the distant sound of hammering. At last Dela turned away as if she would leave—having had enough, I thought: this might wear on for hours. Almost I got to my feet, thinking she might need me—but no, she went only as far as the bench on the other side of the door, drawing Griffin with her, and they sat down there to wait it all out while the crew kept on at their work.

The image came clear finally, and it made no sense, being only dots. "Get the other one up," Modred said, and they started it all over again.

So the crew kept at their work, still getting something, and whatever-it-was kept up its noise. And my lady, who once would have gone to her rooms and shut out the sound—stayed, not even nodding into sleep, but watching every move Modred made.

Not trusting him. Modred had said it. It was very clear why all of us were here, why this one night the lady stayed to witness, and therefore all the rest of us stayed. Modred had to know that.

There had been a time, when the *Maid* had made tame voyages ferrying lovers from star to star, that my lady had liked Modred in contrast at her banquets, with his dark dour ways. He was the shadow in her fancy, the skeleton at the feast, the memento mori—a dangerous-looking sort whose impudence amused her, whose outrages she forgave. But that was before things had passed out of control, and we all had to rely on him. O my lady was afraid of him now, for all the wrong reasons—a grim face, an insolence which had taken matters into his own hands. And a name that had stopped being a joke. He was Modred: she had always had a place for him in her fancy. And so she stopped trusting him.

Me, with my little understanding—I watched him work, the fevered concentration, the sometime flagging of his strength, and the cold, cold patience of his face; and I heard his voice, always quiet, cutting through Percy's dismay at something or Gawain's and Lynn's frustration—like ice it was, beyond disturbance . . . and I knew what it was I feared. I was afraid of his *reasoning*. Modred dealt with our Beast because it was there to be dealt with like the chaos outside, like the numbers that came up on the machinery, a part of this universe and no more alien to his understanding than I was.

But Modred understood now he was not trusted, and he was threatened somehow by that. One little emotion had to be gnawing at him, who could feel nothing else. He had been jolted through a host of sensations in that tape, things his nerves had never felt before. It must have been like a dip in boiling water, leaving no clear impression what the water had been like because the heat was everything.

And what he wanted now, what drove him so, I had no least idea.

The work continued. As with our general terror, information wore us out and left us without reaction—one could only look at so many lines and dots and listen to so much talk that made no particular sense. I found my head nodding, and leaned on Lance, who was more comfortable than the wall; Lance leaned back then and his head bowed over against mine—I went plummeting down a long dark, just too tired to make sense of anything, and the voice of our Beast and the hammering at the hull sang me to sleep.

I came out of it aware of an ache in my neck and of a set of voices in hushed debate.

"No," one said, and: "It's been quiet all this time," the other—Lynn and Modred. "No." Percy's voice. "There's no way—" Gawain's, rising above the level of the others. "Modred, no."

"Lady Dela," Modred said.

I waked thoroughly, sat up as Lance did, as all of us who had been drowsing came awake. Modred looked like death— no sleep, no food or drink but what I had brought him: it showed.

"Lady Dela, it's answered. The transmissions—there's an urgency—" He turned and started touching controls, bringing up a sequence of images, that was all dots and squiggles and lines and circles. "We've rationalized its number system, gotten its chemistry—it's methane. There are all kinds of systems on the wheel—" He brought up another diagram, that was all a jumble of lines, and he pointed to it as my lady and Griffin got to their feet. "There, see—"

"I don't make any sense of it," Dela said.

"There." Modred's hand described a circle: I could see it among the lines when I looked for it, among the other shapes that radiated out from it. And then it made sense—the wheel and the ships appended to it, and the network of tubes that wove them all so that the whole looked like a crown seen from above, with rays and braidings going out in all directions. Modred's thin finger lighted on a single point of this. "This is the *Maid*. Here. Oxygen." His finger underlined a series of dots, and swept to another, impossibly complicated series of dots inside the wheel. "That's methane out there. But here—" His finger swept the torus. "See, there's oxygen, just beyond that partition out there; and a line going that way, from our bow, to that partition. We docked in the wrong segment, and they've corrected that. The torus—has seven divisions. Water, here: they must melt ice. And process other things. Here's a different mix of oxygen; methane/ammonia and sulphur . . ."

"You profess to read this thing's language?"

"A dot code, lady." Modred never looked back, went on showing us his construction—its construction, whosoever it might be. "It's compartmented, various pressures, I'd guess, various temperatures for all its inhabitants. But these—" His hand went to the network of veins. "Methane. All methane. And we may be dealing with a time difference . . . in thought. The creature talking to us sends the images very slowly. But put them together and they animate. Percy—"

Percy ran it back again to earlier images, and we watched, watched the torus naked of ships; and then ships arriving. We watched the network actually grow, watched the lines start from one ship and penetrate the torus, then penetrate the neighboring ship-figure. The dots in it—I had not noticed, but suddenly there were a lot of them.

"Do you see?" Modred asked. "The atmosphere in that ship went to methane. It changed."

But now the lines were going in both directions. New masses popped up, more ships arriving; or asteroids and whole planetoids swept in, docked like ships, because some of the shapes were tiny and some were unaccountably lumpy. Some acquired lines crossing the torus to other sections. I watched, and I felt cold, so that when Lance put his arm about me, I was grateful. Maybe he was cold too. I reached out for Vivien, while the thing went on building, took her cold hand, but she simply stood there with her eyes fixed on the screen and no response at all to my touching her.

So the lines advanced, like blind worms, nodding about and leeching onto a ship-form or a bit of rock; and generally the ships went to that complicated pattern that meant methane. So Modred had said. He watched it grow and grow until the network was mostly about the torus. Until Modred pointed to a ship that suddenly appeared amid the net.

"Ourselves," he said, and the course of it was all but finished except for the waving of the tubes that attached themselves—so, so sinister those thin lines, and the line that appeared leading in another section, and the arrival of another bit of debris far across the wheel . . . something our last jump had swept in, I reckoned.

And Modred looked back at us then. "It's shown us our way out," he said. "We've got to open our forward hatch and go to it."

"O dear God," Dela said with a shake of the head.

"No," Lynette said. "I don't think that's a thing to do that quickly."

"You persist," Modred said, "against the evidence."

"Which can be read other ways," Griffin said. "No."

"Lady Dela," Modred said. Patiently, stone-faced as ever, but his voice was hoarse. "It's a question of profitability. Some of those ships on the ring didn't change. At some points that intrusion failed. And others directly next to them changed. So some do drive it off. There's the tubes, and separately—the wheel itself. It's made an access out to the point where we touch the wheel. We're very close to an oxygen section. Very close to where we should have docked. It can let us through where we have to go."

"Has it occurred to anyone," Vivien asked out of turn, "that however complicated—however attractive and rational and difficult the logical jump it's put us through to reach it— that the thing might *lie?*"

A chill went through me. We looked at one another and for a moment no one had anything to say.

"It's a born-man," Percy said in his soft voice. "Or creature. And so it might lie."

I felt myself paralyzed. And Modred stood there for a moment with a confusion in his eyes, because he was never set up to understand such things—lies, and structures of untruth.

Then he turned and walked toward the main board, just a natural kind of movement, but suddenly everyone seemed to think of it and the crew grabbed for him as Lance and Griffin moved all in the same moment.

Modred lunged, too near to be stopped: his hand hit a control and there was a sound of hydraulics forward before Lance reached past Gawain and Percy and Lynn who pinned Modred to the counter. Lance hauled Modred out and swung him about and hit him hard before Griffin could hinder his arm. Modred hit the floor and slid over under the edge of Gawain's vacant seat, lying sprawled and limp, but Lance would have gone after him, if not for Griffin— And meanwhile Lynette was working frantically at the board, but there had not been a sound of the hydraulics working again.

Our lock was open. Modred had opened us up. The realization got through to Dela and she flew across the deck to Griffin and Lance and the rest of them. "Close it—for God's sake, close it," Dela cried, and I just stood there with my hands to my mouth because it was clear it was not happening.

"It's not working," Lynn said. "Lady Dela, there's something in the doorway and the safety's on—"

"Override," Griffin said.

"There might be some*one* in the way—"

"*Override.*"

Lynn jabbed the button; and all my nerves flinched from

the sound that should have come, maybe cutting some living thing in half— But it failed.

"They've got it braced wide open," Gawain said. "Percy— get cameras down there—"

Percy swung about, and reached the keyboard. All of a sudden we had picture and sound, this hideous babble, this conglomeration of serpent bodies in clear focus—serpents and other things as unlovely, a heaving mass within the *Maid*'s airlock. The second door still held firm, and there was our barrier beyond—there was still that.

"We've got to get down there," Griffin said.

"They can't get through so quickly," Dela said. Her teeth were chattering.

"They don't have to be delicate now they've got that outer lock braced open." Griffin was distraught, his hands on Dela's shoulders. He looked around at all of us. "Suit up. Now. We don't know what they may do. Dela, get to the dining hall and just stay there. And get him out of here—" The latter for Modred, who lay unmoving. "Get him out, locked up, out of our way."

Lance bent down and dragged Modred up. I started to help, took Modred's arm, which was totally limp, as if that great blow had broken him—as if all the fire and drive had just burned him out and Lance's blow had shattered him. For that moment I pitied him, for he never meant to betray us, but he was Modred, made that way and named for it. "Let me," Percivale said, who was much stronger, and who would treat him gently. So I surrendered him to Percivale, to take away, to lock up where he could do us no more harm.

"He'd fight for us," I said to Griffin, thinking that we could hardly spare Modred's wit and his strength, whatever there was left to do now.

"We can't rely on that," Griffin said. He laid his hand on my shoulder, with Dela right there in his other arm. "Elaine—all of you. We do what we planned. All right?"

"Yes, sir," I said, and Gawain the same. A silence from Vivien.

"Come on," Griffin said.

So we went, and now over com we could hear the sound of what had gotten into the ship. I imagined them calling for cutters in their hisses and their squeals, and scaly dragon bodies pressing forward—oh, it could happen quickly now, and my skin drew as if there had been a cold wind blowing.

No sound of trumpets. No brave charge. We had armor, but it was all too fragile, and swords, but they had lasers, all too likely; and all the history of this place was theirs, not ours.

A land of old upheaven from the abyss
By fire, to sink into the abyss again;
Where fragments of forgotten peoples dwelt,
And the long mountains ended in a coast
Of ever-shifting sand, and far away
The phantom circle of a moaning sea.
. . . And there, that day when the great light of heaven
Burned at his lowest in the rolling year,
On the waste sand by the waste sea they closed.
Nor yet had Arthur fought a fight
Like this last, dim, weird battle of the west.
A deathwhite mist slept over sand and sea:
Whereof the chill, to him who breathed it, drew
Down with his blood, till all his heart was cold
With formless fear; and ev'n on Arthur fell
Confusion, since he saw not whom he fought.
For friend and foe were shadows in the mist,
And friend slew friend not knowing whom he slew.

XV

We had put the suits all in the dining room, all piled in the
corner like so many bodies; and the breathing units were by
them in a stack; and the helmets by those. . . . "Shouldn't
we," I said, taking my lady's suit from Percy, who was dis-
tributing pieces. I turned to my lady. "—shouldn't we take
Modred's to him—in case?"

"No," Griffin said behind me, and firmly. "He'll be safe
enough only so he stays put."

I doubted that. I doubted it for all of us, and it seemed
cruel to me. But I helped my lady with her suit, which she
had never put on before, and which I had never tried. Lance

was helping Griffin with his; but Lynn and Gawain had to intervene with both of us to help because they knew the fittings and where things should go and we did not.

Griffin was first done, knowing himself something about suits and getting into them. He had his helmet in his hand and waved off assistance from Gawain. "Dela," he said then, "you stay here. You can't help down there, you hear me?"

"I hear you," she said, "but I'm coming down there anyway."

"Dela—"

"I'll stay back," she said, "but I'll be behind you."

Griffin looked distraught. He wanted to say no again, that was sure; but he turned then and took one of the swords in hand, his helmet tucked under his arm. "There'll be no using the beam cutters or the explosives," he said. "If that's methane out there. Modred did us that much service. So the swords and spears are all we've got. Dela—" Maybe he had something more to say and changed his mind. He lost it, whatever it had been, and walked off and out the door while we worked frantically at my lady's fastenings.

"Hurry," Dela insisted, and Lynette got the last clip fastened.

"Done," Lynn said, and my lady, moving carefully in the weight, took her helmet from my hands and tucked that up, then gathered up several of the spears.

"Vivien," my lady said sharply, and fixed Viv with her eye, because Viv was standing against the wall with never a move to do anything. "You want to wait here until they come slithering up the halls, Vivien?"

"No, lady," Vivien said, and went and took the suit that Percy offered her.

"Help me," Viv said to us. She meant it as an order. But my lady was already headed out the door, and Lance and I were in no frame of mind to wait on Vivien.

"Get us ready," I said to Lynn and Gawain. "Hurry. Hurry. They're alone down there."

But Percivale delayed his own suiting to attend to Vivien, who was all but shivering with fright. I heard the lift work a second time and knew my lady had gone without us . . . and still we had that sound everywhere. Lynn batted my overanxious hands from the fastenings and did them the way they should be done, and settled the weight of the lifesupport on

me so that I felt my knees buckle; and fastened that with
snaps of catches. "Go," she said then, and I bent gingerly to
get my helmet and took another several of the spears. But
Lance took a sword the same as Griffin's, and a spear besides.
He moved as if that great weight of the suit were nothing to
him. He strode out and down the corridor, and I followed after him as best I could, panting and trying not to catch a
spearpoint on the lighting fixtures of the walls.

I had no intention that he should wait; if he could get to
the lift and get down there the faster, so much the better, but
he held the lift for me and shouted at me to hurry, so I came,
with the shuffling haste I could manage, and I got myself and
my unwieldly load into the lift and leaned against the wall as
he hit the button with his gloved knuckles. It dropped us
down that two deck distance and the door opened on a hideous din of thumps and bangs, but remoter than I had feared.

My lady was there, and Griffin. They stood hand in hand
in front of the welded barrier, their weapons set aside, and
they looked glad to see us as we came.

"Elaine," Griffin said right off, "your job is to protect your
lady, you understand. You stay beside her whatever happens."

"Yes, sir," I said.

"And Lance," he said, "I need you."

"Yes, sir," Lance said without quibble, because it meant
being up front beyond a doubt, with all our hopes in defense
of all of us.

"They're not through the airlock yet," Dela said. "They're
working at it."

"When our atmospheres mix," Griffin said, "we're in danger
of blowing everything. At least they know. I imagine they'll
use some kind of a pressure gate and do the cut in an oxygen
mix. If they've got suits, and I'm betting they do."

"We could set up a defense on next level," Lance said.

"Same danger there; they convert this level to their own atmosphere, then we've got it all over again. Our whole
lifesupport bled out into all that methane would diffuse too
much for any danger; but if they let all that methane in
here—it could blow the ship apart. A quick way out. There's
that. We could always touch it off ourselves."

"Griffin," Dela said.

"If we had to."

I felt cold, that was all, cold all the way inside, despite that carrying the suit made me sweat.

The lift worked. Vivien came, alone, walking with difficulty, and she had gotten herself one of the spears, carrying that in one hand, and her helmet under the other arm. She joined us.

And the lift went up and came down again with Gawain and Lynn and Percy, who moved better with their suits than the rest of us. They had swords and spears, and some of the knives with them.

"We wait," Griffin said.

So we got down on our knees, that being the only way to sit down in the suits, and I only hoped we should have a great deal of warning when the attack came, because even the strongest of us were clumsy, down on one knee and then the other, and then sitting more or less sideways. I was all but panting, and I felt sweat run under the suit, but my legs felt the relief, and finding a way to rest the corner of the lifesupport unit against the deck gave me delirious relief from the weight.

Bang. Thump.

Be careful, Beast, I thought at it, imagining all its minions and ourselves blown to atoms, to drift and swirl out there amongst the chaos-stuff. In one part of my mind—I think it was listening to the wrong kind of tapes—I was glad of a chance like that, that we might do some terrible damage to our attackers and maybe put a hole in the side of the wheel that they would remember . . . all, all those scaly bodies going hurtling out amongst our fragments.

But in the saner part of my mind I did not want to die.

And oh, if they should get their hands on us. . . . Hands. If they had hands at all. If they thought anything close to what we thought.

If, if, and if. Bang. Thump. Griffin and my lady told stories—recollected a day at Brahmani Dali, and smiled at each other. "I love you," Griffin said then to Dela, a sober, afterthinking kind of voice, meaning it. I knew. I focused beyond them at Lance, and his face looked only troubled as all our faces did. It was no news to him, not now.

So we sat, and shifted our weight because the waiting grew long.

"They could take days about it," Dela said.

"I doubt it," Griffin said.

"They'll suit up," Gawain said. "They'll have that weight to carry, just like us."

"I wish they'd get on about it." That plaintive voice from Vivien. Her eyes were very large in the dim light of the corridor, where the makeshift bulkhead had cut off some of the lighting. "What can they be doing out there?"

"Likely assuring their own safety."

"They can't come at us with firearms," Lynn said. "If we can't use them, they daren't."

"That's so," Dela breathed.

"Not at close range," Griffin said. He laughed. "Maybe they're hunting up weapons like ours."

That would be a wonder, I thought. I was encouraged by the thought—until I reckoned that the odds were still likely theirs and not ours. And then the realization settled on me darker and heavier than before, for that little breath of hope, that we really had no hope at all, and that we only did this for—

When I thought of it, I couldn't answer why we tried. For our born-men, that was very simple . . . and not so simple, if there was no hope. It was not in our tapes—to fight. But here was even Vivien, clutching a spear across her knees, when I *knew* her tapes were hardly set that way. They made us out of born-man material, and perhaps, the thought occurred to me, that somewhere at base they and we were not so different—that born-men would do things because it leapt into their minds to do them, like instincts inherent in the flesh.

Or the tapes we had stolen had muddled us beyond recall.

The sound stopped again, close to us, though it kept on above. "They've arranged something, maybe," Dela said. "God help us."

"Easy," Griffin said. And: "When it comes—understand, Dela, you and Elaine and Vivien take your position back just ahead of the crosspassage. If anything gets past us you take care of it."

"Right," Dela said.

If. It seemed to me a very likely if, recalling that flood of bodies I had seen within our lock.

But the silence went on.

"Lady Dela," Percy said then, very softly.

Dela looked toward him.

"Lady Dela, you being a born-man—do you talk to God?"

My heart turned over in me. Viv's head came up, and Lance's and Gawain's and Lynn's. We all froze.

"God?" Dela asked.

"Could you explain," Percivale went on doggedly, stammering on so dreadful an impertinence, "could you say —whether if we die we have souls? Or if God can find them here."

"Percy," Viv said sharply. "Somebody—Percy—"

Shut him up, she meant—right for once; and I put out my hand and tugged at his arm, and Lance pulled at him, but Percy was not to be stopped in this. "My lady—" he said.

My lady had the strangest look on her face—thinking, looking at all of us—and we all stopped moving, almost stopped breathing for Percy's sake. She would hurt him, I thought; I was sure. But she only looked perplexed. "Who put that into your head?" she asked.

No one said, least of all Percy, whose face was very pale. No one said anything for a very long time.

"Do you know, lady?" Percy asked.

"Dear God, what's happened to you?"

"I—" Percy said. But it got no further than that.

"He took a tape," Vivien said. "He's never been the same since."

"It was me," I said, because she left me nothing more to say. "It was the tape—The tape." I knew she understood me then, and her eyes had turned to me. "It was never Percy's fault. He only borrowed it from me, not knowing he should never have it. We—all . . . had it. It was an accident, lady Dela. But my fault."

Her eyes were still fixed on me, in such stark dismay—and then she looked from me to Lance, and Gawain and Lynette and Vivien and Griffin and last to Percivale, as if she were seeing us for the first time, as if suddenly she knew us. The dream settled about us then, wrapped her and Griffin too.

"Percivale," she said, with a strange gentleness, "I've no doubt of you."

I would have given much for such a look from my lady. I know that Lance would have. And perhaps even Vivien. We were forgiven, I thought. And it was if a great weight left us all at once, and we were free.

Vivien, whose spite had spilled it all—looked taken aback,

as if she had run out of venom, as if she found a kind of dismay in what she was made to be. Maybe she grew a little then. At least she had nothing more to say.

And then a new sound, a groaning of machinery, that clanked and rattled and of a sudden a horrid rending of metal.

"O my God," Dela breathed.

"Steady. All of you."

"They've got the lock," Lynn surmised. And a moment more and we knew that, because there was a rumbling and clanking closer and closer to the makeshift bulkhead behind which we sat. I clenched my handful of spears, ready when Griffin should say the word.

"Helmets," he said, reaching for his.

I dropped the spears and picked up my lady's, to help her, small skill that I had. But Percy took it from my hands, quick and sure, and helped her, as Lynn helped me. The helmet frightened me—cutting me off from the world, like that white place of my nightmares. But the air flowed and it was cooler than the air outside, and Lynn took my hand and pressed it on a control at my chest so that I could hear her voice.

". . . your com," she said. "Keep it on."

I heard other voices, Lance's and Griffin's as they got their helmets on and got to their feet. Griffin helped Dela stand and Percy got me on my feet so that I could lean on my spears and stay there. Everything was very distant: the helmet which had seemed for a moment to cut off all the familiar world from me now seemed instead to contain it, the cooling air, the voices of my comrades. It was insulation from the horrid sounds of them advancing against our last fortification, so that we went surrounded in peace.

"Get back," Griffin said; and Dela reached out her hand for his and leaned against him only the moment—two white-suited ungainly figures, one very tall and the other more suit and lifepack than woman. "Take care of her," Griffin wished us, all calm in the stillness that went about us.

"Yes, sir," I said. "We will." We meaning Viv and I. And Dela came with us, a slow retreat down the corridor, so as not to tire ourselves, the three of us armed with spears. Dela kept delaying to turn and look back again, but I didn't look, not until we had reached the place where we should stand, and then I maneuvered my thickly booted feet about and saw

Lance and Griffin and the crew who had determined where *they* would stand, not far behind the bulkhead. Their backs were to us. They had their swords and a few weighted pipes that Gawain and Lynn had brought down, and a spear or two. They stood two and three, Lance and Griffin to the fore and the crew behind. And I felt vibration through my boots, and heard their voices discussing it through the suit com, because they had felt it too.

"It won't be long," Griffin said. "We go forward if we can. We push them out the lock and get it sealed."

"They may have prevented that," Gawain said, "if they jammed something into the track."

"We do what we can," Griffin said.

Myself, I thought how those creatures had gotten up against us, and wrenched the second door apart with the sound of metal rending, a lock that was meant to withstand fearful stress. Modred's had been a small betrayal; it lost us little. They could easily have torn us open—when they wished, when they were absolutely ready.

"Feel it?" Dela asked.

"Yes," I said, knowing she meant the shuddering through the floor.

"They can't stop them," Viv said.

"Then it's our job," I said, "isn't it?"

The whole floor quivered, and we *felt* the sound, as suddenly there was a squeal of tearing metal that got even through the insulating helmets. Light glared round the edges of the bulkhead where it met the overhead, and widened, irregularly, all with this wrenching protest of bending metal, until all at once the bulkhead gave way on other sides, and drew back, showing a glare of white light beyond. The bulkhead was being dragged back and back with a terrible rumbling, a jolting and uncertainty until it dropped and fell flat with a jarring boom. A head on a long neck loomed in its place. For a moment I thought it alive; and so I think did Griffin and the rest, who stood there in what was now an open access—but it was machinery silhouetted against the glare of floods, our longnecked dragon nothing but a thing like a piston pulling backward, contracting into itself, so that now we saw the ruined lock, and the flare of lights in smoke or fog beyond that.

"Machinery," I heard Lance say.

But what came then was not—a sinuous plunge of bodies through the haze of light and fog, like a cresting wave of serpent-shadows hurling themselves forward into the space the machinery had left.

My comrades shouted, a din in my ears: *"Come on!"* That was Griffin: he took what ground there was to gain, he and Lance—and Gawain and Lynn and Percy behind them, two and then three more human shadows heading into the wreckage and the fog, tangling themselves with the coming flood.

"Come *on*," my lady said, and meant to keep our interval: I came, hearing the others' sounds of breath and fighting—heard Griffin's voice and Lance's, and Lynn who swore like a born-man and yelled at Gawain to watch out. We ran forward as best we could, behind the others. "No!" I heard Viv wail, but I paid no attention, staying with my lady.

And oh, my comrades bought us ground. Shadows in the mist, they cut and hewed their way with sobs for breath that we could hear, and no creature got by them, but none died either. We crossed the threshold of the ruined bulkhead, and now Griffin pushed the fight into the lock itself, still driving them back. "Wait," I heard, Viv's voice. "Wait for me." But Dela and I kept on, picking our way over the wreckage of the fallen bulkhead, then past the jagged edges of the torn inner lock.

And then they carried the fight beyond the lock, in a battle we could not see . . . driving the serpent-shapes outside.

But when we had come into the lock, my lady and I, and Vivien panting behind us—it was all changed, everything. I knew what we *should* see—an access tube, a walkway, something the like of which we had known at stations; but we stared into lights, and steam or some milky stuff roiled about, making shadows of our folk and the serpents, and taller, upright shapes behind, like a war against giants, all within a ribbed and translucent tube that stretched on and on in violet haze. "Look out!" I heard Lance cry, and then: "Percy!"

And from Lynette: "He's down—"

"Dela—" Griffin's voice. "Dela—"

"I'm here," she said, wanting to go forward, but I held her arm. They had all they could handle, Griffin and the rest.

"Fall back," I heard him say. "We can't go this—Get Percy up; get back."

They were retreating of a sudden as the other, taller shapes

pressed on them like an advancing wall. I heard Gawain urg-
ing Percy up; saw the retreat of two figures, and the slower
retreat of three. "Back up," Griffin ordered, out of breath,
and then: "Watch it!"

Suddenly I lost sight of them in a press of bodies. I heard
confused shouting, not least of it Dela's voice crying out after
Griffin; and Gawain and Percy were yelling after Lance and
Griffin both.

But still Griffin's voice, swearing and panting at once, and
then: "You can't—Lance, get back, get back.—*Dela!*—Dela,
I'm in trouble. I can't get loose—Modred—Get Modred—"

"Modred," Dela said. She turned on me and seized my arm
and shook at me so that I swung round and looked into her
eyes through the double transparency of the helmets. "Let
him loose—let Modred loose, hear?"

I understood. I gave her my spear and I plunged back past
Viv, back through the lock again and over the debris—no
questioning; and still in my suit com I could hear my comrades' anguished breaths and sometimes what I thought was
Lance, a kind of a sobbing that was like a man swinging a
weight, a sword, and again and fainter still . . . Griffin's
voice, and louder—Dela's.

"Get them back," I heard. That was Lance for sure; and
an oath: that was Lynette.

I had the awful sights in my eyes even while I was feeling
my overweighted way over the debris in the corridors; and
then my own breath was sobbing so loud and my heart
pounding so with my struggle to run that the sounds dimmed
in my ears. I reached the open corridor; I ran in shuffling
steps; I made the lift and I punched the buttons with thick
gloved fingers, knees buckling under the thrust of the car as it
rose, one level, another. Up here too I could hear a sound
. . . a steady sound through the walls, that was another attack at us, another breaching of the *Maid*'s defense.

Get Modred. There was no one else who might defend the
inner ship, and that was all we had left. I knew, the same as
my lady knew, and I got out into the corridor topside and
shuffled my clumsy way down it with my comrades' voices
dimmed altogether now, and only my own breaths for company.

I pushed the button, opening it. Modred had heard me
coming—how could he not? He was standing there, a black

figure, just waiting for me, and when I gestured toward the bridge he cut me off with a shove that thrust me out of the way . . . ran, the direction of the bridge, free to do what he liked.

"Go," his voice reached me over com, in short order, but I was already doing that, knowing where I belonged. "Elaine . . . get everyone out of the corridors."

"Modred," Dela said, far away and faint. "We're holding here . . . at the lock. We've lost Griffin—"

"Get out of the corridors," he said. "Quickly."

I made the lift. I rode it down, into the depths and the glare of lights beyond the ruined corridor. They might have taken it by now, I was thinking . . . I might meet the serpent shapes the instant the door should open; but that would mean all my friends were gone, and I rushed out the door with all the force I could muster, seeing then a cluster of human shapes beyond the debris, three standing, two kneeling, and I heard nothing over com.

"My lady," I breathed, coming as quickly as I could.

"Elaine," I heard . . . her voice. And one of the figures by her was very tall, who turned beside my lady as I reached them.

Lance and my lady and Vivien; and Gawain and Lynette kneeling over Percivale, who had one arm clamped tight to his chest, his right. But of Griffin there was no sign; and in the distance the ranks of the enemy heaved and surged, shadows beyond the floods they had set up in the tube.

"Modred's at controls," I said, asking no questions. "He'll do what he can." And because I had to: "I think they're about to break through up there."

My lady said nothing. No one had anything to say.

Modred would do what was reasonable. Of that I had no least doubt. If there was anything left to do. We were defeated. We knew that, when we had lost Griffin. And so Dela let Modred loose, the other force among us.

"Lady Dela," Modred's voice came then. "I suggest you come inside and seal yourselves into a compartment."

"I suggest you do something," Dela said shortly. "That's what you're there for."

"Yes, my lady," Modred said after a moment, and there was a squealing in the background. "But we're losing pressure in the topside lab. I think they're venting our lifesupport. I'd really suggest you take what precautions you can, immediately."

"We hold the airlock," Dela said.

"No," Modred said. "You can't." A second squealing, whether of metal or some other sound was uncertain.

And then the com went out.

"Modred?" Dela said. "Modred, answer me."

"We've lost the ship," Lynette said.

"Lady Dela—" Lance said quietly. "They're moving again."

They were. Toward us. A wall of serpents and taller shapes like giants, lumpish, in what might be suits or the strangeness of their own bodies.

Dela stopped and gathered up a spear, leaned on it, cumbersome in her suit. "Get me up," Percy was saying. "Get me on my feet."

"If they want the ship," Dela said then in a voice that came close to trembling, "well, so they have it. We fall aside and if we can we go right past their backs. We go the direction they took Griffin, hear?"

"Yes," Lance said. Gawain got Percy on his feet. He manged to stay there. Lynette stood up with me and Vivien. Out of Vivien, not a word, but she still held her spear, and it struck me then that she had not blanked: for once in a crisis Vivien was still around, still functioning. Born-man tapes had done that much for her.

The lines advanced, more and more rapidly, a surge of serpent bodies, a waddle of those behind, beyond the hulking shape of the machinery they had used to breach us, past the glare of the floods.

But now farewell. I am going a long way
With those thou seest—if indeed I go—
For all my mind is clouded with a doubt—
To the island-valley of Avilion.

XVI

So we stood. In front of us was that machine like a ram, and that was a formidable thing in itself; but it was frozen dead. And about it was a fog, a mist that made it hard to see—I thought it must be of their devising, to mask how many they were, or what they did, or prepared to do. Within the mist we could see red serpent shapes shifting position, weaving their bodies together like restless braiding, like grass in a sideways wind, like coursers held at a starting mark, eager and restrained. It was peculiarly horrible, that constant action; and broadbodied giants stood behind, purplish shadows less distinct, an immobile hedge like a fortification.

"You understand," said my lady Dela, "that when they come, we only seem to hold; and fall aside and lie low until we can get behind their lines. Don't try more than that. Does everyone understand?"

We avowed that we did, each answering.

And then a clearer, different voice, that was from the *Maid*'s powerful system. "My lady Dela." Modred. And a sound behind his voice like groaning metal, like—when the lock had given way. "I've sealed upper decks. They're breaking through the seal. I suggest you withdraw inside. Now."

"My orders stand," Dela said.

"There's danger of explosion, lady Dela. Come inside *now*. I am in contact with the alien. It instructs we give access."

177

"Protect the ship."

"I'm doing that."

"You take your orders from me, Modred."

A silence. A squeal of metal.

"Modred?"

"They're in. We've lost all upper deck. Withdraw into the ship."

And now it began. In front of us. The serpents were loosed, and they came, looping and heaving forward like the breaking of a reddish wave. The giants behind them moved like a living wall.

"Stand still," Dela said, paying no more heed to Modred. Lance and Lynette put themselves in front of her, and Percy and Gawain stood to either side. Myself, I gripped my spear in thick gloved hands and left Viv behind us, moved up to Percy's side, because his one arm was useless now.

Oh, there was not enough time, no time at all to get used to this idea. I had never hit anything. I had a sudden queasiness in my stomach like psych-sets amiss, but it was raw fear, a doubt of what I was doing, to fall under that alien mass—but that was what our lady had said we must do.

"They're hard to cut," I heard Lance tell us; very calm, Lance, my lady's sometime lover and never meant for more. "But hit them. They do feel it."

They. I could see them clearly now. The serpents had legs and used them, poured forward overrunning their own slower members, like the rolling of a sea, all soundless in the insulation of my helmet, and time slowed down as my mind began to take in all of this detail, as my heart beat and my hands realized a weapon in them. The tide reached Lance and Lynette and boiled about them, hip-high until they felt Lance's blows. One reared up, and others, and those behind overran, climbing the rearing bodies, with blind nodding heads, and flung themselves aside and poured past. One came at me, a snaky, legged body whose hide was a slick membrane of purples and reds. I swallowed bile and jabbed at it with all my strength: the point of the spear made a dent in its muscle and scored its slickish hide: it nodded its head this way and that in eyeless pain: a small *O* of a mouth opened and its screaming reached me past my comrades' amplified sobs for breath and my lady's curses. I had no idea what became of that beast or where it went: there was another and I struck at that, and went on jabbing and beating at them until my joints ached, until finally one slithered behind my legs and another slid off an attacking body and came down in my face, huge and heavy and horridly alive.

I was buried in such bodies. I yelled out for horror, bruised, aghast at the writhing under and over me as I became flotsam in that alien tide. "My lady!" I cried, and heard someone cry out in great pain—O Percy! I thought then, with his arm already torn; and where my comrades were in this or where my lady was I could not see. Even the light was cut off, as a body pressed over my faceplate, and then my com went out, so that I had only my own voice inside my helmet, and the murmuring rush from outside.

Then the mass above flowed off me, and I saw light— saw—the giants passing near, next in the alien ranks. One almost trod on me, indifferent, and I clawed my way aside, scrambled atop that heaving mass of dragon-shapes, tumbled then, borne toward the *Maid*'s gaping lock. I remembered the com control on my chest, pressed the button and had sound again, Lance's deep voice calling out a warning: "Look *out!*"

And oh—the giants were not the worst, them with their broad violet bodies like gnarled trees come to life— There was a shape that shuffled along as if it herded them all, a lumpish thing larger even than they, and puffed with delicate veined bladders about its face, its—I could not see that it had limbs in its fluttering membranous folds. It seemed brown; but the membranes shaded off to greens, to—blues about its center and golds about its extremities. It rippled as it moved. There was a wholeness and power about it that—in all its horror— was symmetry.

I saw one of us gain his feet, sword in both his hands. It was Lance: I heard his voice calling after help even while he swung at it to drive it off. Its membranes fluttered with the cuts. I scrambled over bodies to gain my feet; I saw another of us closer, trying to help; but it came on, and on—just spread itself wider and gathered Lance in sword and all; and that other, who must be Gawain—it got him too, and it kept coming, at me. I couldn't find my spear; but of a sudden my feet met bare decking, the serpents all fled as the fleshy webs spread about me, all dusky now: more limbs/segments—I saw the floods glow like murky suns through the folds as it swept about me. I felt—horror—muscle within those folds, a solid center. I heard one of my friends cry out; I heard some-one curse.

And it *spoke* to us—our Beast: it was nothing else but that. It rumbled deep within and moaned and ticked at us, a sound that quivered through my frame until it was beyond bearing. I yelled back at it—*I* screamed at it, till my throat hurt and my voice broke. I heard nothing. The sound pierced my teeth and marrow, too deep for hearing.

I hit the flooring on my back suddenly, which for all my lifesupport and padding hardly more than jolted me. The veil of its limbs swept on, the sound was gone, and it passed, leaving me lying amid the litter of our weapons. I flailed about getting over on my knees so that I could begin to get up. I heard Viv making a strange lost sound, but she was there. And my lady—"Lady Dela," I called, trying to reach her to help; but Lance was first, pulling her to her feet. A hand helped me, and steadied me, and that was Gawain. Percy—I looked about, and he was on his feet, with Lynette. I found my spear, or someone's, and gathered it up. Our Beast lumbered on, into the *Maid*'s open airlock, as all the rest had done, leaving us alone.

"Modred," Gawain cried, and he would have gone after, but Lance caught his arm. And Lynette:

"My lady," she said then, and pointed with her sword the way toward the machine, the way down the passage, that we had hoped to go.

And there amid the smokes stood another rank of giants, no less than the first.

Dela swayed on her feet. The weight we all carried seemed suddenly too much for her. "We've lost," she said. "Haven't we?" And slowly she turned toward us. I couldn't see her face: our faceplates only reflected each other, featureless. "Percivale," she said, "is the arm broken?"

"My lady," he said, "I think it is."

She was silent for a moment. "So we've nowhere to go." She bent down. I thought she meant to sit down. But she picked up a spear from off the ground and stood up and faced toward the giants.

So did we all then. It was that simple. It occurred to me fi-nally that my knees hurt and I was bruised and sore from that battering, when my heart had settled down, when the minutes wore on. One of us sat down, slow settling to the deck. We looked; and that was Viv, sitting there, but not blanked . . . "Vivien," my lady asked, "are you all right?"

"Yes, lady," Viv said, a small thin voice. She was with us. She had her spear in both her hands. She was just never very strong, except in will. She wanted to live. She fought for that, perhaps. Perhaps it was something less noble. With Vivien I never knew.

But she was there.

It was a strange thing, that none of the rest of us sat down, when it was so much more reasonable to do. When giving up, I suppose, was reasonable. But getting up took so long a time, and we had seen how fast the enemy could move. Besides— besides, there was a sense in us that it was not a thing to do, facing this thing. My hands clenched tight about the spear and while I had no strength to go charging at them, I wished they would come on so that I could do something with this frustration that was boiling in me . . . in *me*, who could feel such a thing.

We should have the banner here, I thought. We should have the bright true colors, which was what we *were*, in this place of violet murk and white mist and glaring floods. It might be they would understand us then—what we meant, standing here. Maybe others besides humans used such symbols. Maybe it would only puzzle them. Or maybe they would think it a message where voices meant nothing at all, one side to the other.

But we had nothing. We had no faces to them; and they had none for us, standing like a wall of trees.

And silent.

"*Ah!*" Vivien cried, a sudden gasp of horror from behind us. I jerked about, nextmost to her—a serpent was among us, loping from out the lock. Vivien hurled herself aside from it, and I did, thoroughly startled; but as I turned to see it pass, Gawain hit it with his sword. It writhed aside and scuttled through with all its speed, evading Lance and my lady and Lynette, running as hard as it could go toward the cover of the machine and its waiting giant comrades.

"A messenger," Dela said. "We should have stopped it."

"*My lady*—" A faint voice, static-riddled.

"Modred," Dela exclaimed. "Modred, we hear you."

"It . . . inside . . . the tubes . . . I don't . . ."

"Modred?"

". . . broken through . . ."

"*Modred.*"

". . . tried . . ."

And then static overwhelmed the voice.

"I think," said Lynette, "that's a suit com."

"Modred," Dela said, "keep talking."

But we got nothing but static back.

"If he's still near controls," Percy said, his voice very thin and strained, "he may be communicating with the other side."

I cast an encumbered look toward the line of giants, fearing *that* coming at our backs. "My lady," I said, "they're closer."

Others looked as I looked back; and then—"The lock!" Percy exclaimed.

It was back, our Beast. It filled the doorway, having to deflate some of its bladders to pass the door; and in leathery limbs like an animal's limbs it had something white clutched against it and buried in its membranes.

"Modred," Dela exclaimed in horror.

He looked dead, crushed and still. And the bladders inflated again, in all their murky shades of blue, taking him from view. But then the limbs unfolded and it squatted and let him to the decking, a sprawl of a white-suited figure out of that dreadful alien shape. It spoke to us, a loud rumbling that vibrated from the deck into our bones; and oh, what it was to be held inside it when it spoke, with the sound shaking brain and marrow. It stood over Modred, partly covering him with its membranes. It quivered and rumbled and wailed and ticked, and Lance came at it, not really an attack, but making it know he would. I moved, and the others did; and the giants were a shadow very close to us, coming at our side.

Then our Beast retreated, a flowing away from us toward the giants, a nodding, slow withdrawal, and rumbling and ticking all the while. A loping serpent, murky red, came out of the lock and ran along beside it as it went.

And Modred stirred, alive and making small motions toward getting up. "Oh, help him," I asked my friends, but I was closest besides Lance, and I bent and went down to one knee as best I could, so that Modred found my other knee and levered himself up. He touched his chest, got his com working, but his head was turned toward the Beast in its slow retreat toward the giants, who had stopped in their advance. I only heard Modred's breathing, that came in gasps. And somehow the hinder view of the Beast looked more human-like in shadow, like a slump-shouldered giant shuffling away, its monster serpent looping along beside it like some fawning pet, ignored in its master's melancholy.

"It's the oldest," Modred said. "The captain of the core object . . . first here. Unique."

"You called it here," my lady said, accusing him. "You brought this on, all of it."

"No," Modred said. "It had to come. There were the tubes."

Sometimes Modred failed to make sense. And sometimes I feared I understood him after all.

"They took Griffin," Dela cried, with a sweep of her hand in the direction of the retreating Beast. "They took him away with them."

A lift of Modred's head. "I think I know where."

That struck my lady silent. I looked up, past her, past Lance, where this creature, this shuffling monster passed behind the giant ranks and disappeared. *They* stayed, beside the giant ram, indistinct in the fog they had made. But they came no nearer.

"The tubes," Modred said indistinctly. "They had to get us out of the way . . . the *Maid's* filled with methane now, where they can carry the fight into the tubes themselves; but we're to follow the passage to the next sector. That's where they'll have taken him, most probably."

"Did they tell you that?" My lady's voice was still and careful, edged and hard. "Do you carry on dialogues, you and that thing?"

"It was in the map," Modred said.

A silence then. My heart hurt, from fear. From—I had no notion what. I was shivering. Maybe Modred was mad. Or maybe we had all lost ourselves in a dream, and we had forgotten what he was.

"He did the best he knew," I said for him. "He tried not to be Modred, lady Dela. He really tried. He did."

"Down the passage," Dela said then. "So we hand ourselves over to them?"

We thought about that.

"I'll go," Lance said quietly. "And come back again if I can."

"No," Dela said. "We'll all go.—Modred, can you walk?"

He pressed hard on my knee trying to get up. Gawain helped him, steadying him with an arm; and then Lynette had to help me, because I just hadn't the strength left to straighten my leg and lift the weight of my suit. She held me on my feet a moment until I had my breath and got my feet braced. What held Percy on his feet—he was not large or so strong as Lance—I had no idea. And Lynette helped Vivien up next.

"We can't go through that," Vivien protested, meaning the giants, who stood like a murky wall in front of us. Her voice shook. I took her hand that still held the spear and pressed her gloved fingers about the shaft, set the butt of it firmly on the decking.

I said nothing. With Viv that was usually safest. "Come on," Dela said, and so we went, all of us, with what strength we had.

Then from the dawn it seem'd there came, but faint
As from beyond the limit of the world,
Like the last echo born of a great cry,
Sounds, as if some fair city were one voice
Around a king returning from his wars.

XVII

There was no suddenness in this encounter. The giants stood, and we—we came as best we could, at the little pace that the least of us could manage. Lance was first of us, strongest, and Vivien trailed last. Breath sounded loud in my ears, mine, my comrades', while the giants loomed closer still; and over us as we passed by the huge machinery, amid the smoke.

"Stay together," Dela said, because for that moment we couldn't see at all, except the white mist about us, with the glare of lights, and sometimes a shadow that might be one of us or the movement of some creature in ambush there.

A shape came clear to me, like a pillar in the murk and going up and up; and this was the leg of one of the giants, armored by nature or wearing some kind of suit different than ours. I shied from it and shied the other way at once, about to collide with another. I had lost my comrades. In the helmet I had no sense of direction. I plunged ahead the way that I thought I had been going, blind, among these monstrous shapes.

And they ignored us as we passed, never stirred, unless those vast heads looked down with slight curiosity and wondered what we were. We passed through the mist and I saw my lady and Lance and Lynette; looked back and I saw

Gawain and Modred coming out from the mist; then another that was Vivien, by the size.

"Percy," I called.

"I'm here," he answered me, hoarse and faint. I saw one more of us clear the mist and follow, and I let Viv pass me, delayed to walk with Percy, not to lose him again.

"I'll make it," he said, but that was only to keep me happy: none of us knew where we were going or how far . . . except maybe Modred, who limped along in our midst.

And ahead of us stretched more and more of the passage, which bent gently rightward, and the way was dim, violet shadowed, once we were past the floods and the mist. "My lady," Lynette said from up ahead, "we could use the suit lights, but I don't think we should."

"No," Dela agreed, hard-breathing. "We don't need more attention than we have."

"They don't care," Modred said faintly. "They could have stopped us if they had."

No one answered. No one had Modred's confidence. And even his sounded shaken.

The shadows deepened. The way branched left, toward a vast sealed hatch; and right, toward more passageway. We walked toward that choice, saying nothing, only breathing in one breath, a unison of exhaustion, mine, my lady's, everyone's. Lance and Lynette stopped there, stood and looked back until we had come closer.

"Bear right," Modred said, between his breaths, and gestured toward the open passage.

"Go right," my lady said after a moment, and herself began to walk again. So we all did, getting our weighted bodies into reluctant motion. I saw Vivien falter; she used her spear like a staff now, to keep herself steady, and leaned on it and kept moving. We walked slower and slower through the murk.

Until the second door, that closed off the way ahead, another hatch vast as the first, everything on giant scale.

We caught up to one another, and Lynn turned on a light, that she played over the huge machinery of the lock, but I saw no control, no panel, nothing in our reach.

Lance struck it a blow with his sword, frustration if nothing else.

And it shot apart, two sideways jaws gaping with a rumble

that shook the deck under us, showing murky dark inside, a second steel door. My heart stopped and started again, faltering; my lady called on God; and someone had cried out. Then:

"Come on," my lady said, and the first of us went in. Vivien delayed, in front of Percivale and me. "Move, Viv," I said, and Percivale just took Viv's arm in his good hand, and I took the other, so we kept up.

I knew that those doors would close again with us inside. They must. It was a lock. And they did, when we were barely across the threshold, a thunder at our heels, a shock that swayed us on our feet, and a machine-sound after, like pumps working. I flinched, and Viv jerked, but kept her feet.

Then the inner doors thundered back, and we blinked in brighter light, in light like sunshine, and an impression of green.

"Oh," my lady said, very quietly, and I shivered where I stood, because it was a world we faced, a land, an upward-curving horizon hazing into misty distances, with a vast central lake that disappeared in an overhead glare of lighting far above.

That was not all. Things moved here, from either side of us at once—tall creatures, gangling, clothed, some brown skinned and some azure-blue, some red-furred; and all armed, taking up a defensive line.

And they had Griffin with them—suitless, unrestrained.

"Griffin," my lady cried. And threw down her spear and went to him, trying all the while to rid herself of the helmet.

He knew her at once. There was none of us so small as she was; he flung his arms about her, and helped her with the helmet then, so we all knew it was safe.

The crew knew how; it took Gawain's help for my helmet and Lance's and Viv's. We stood there, having let our weapons fall, while my lady and master Griffin were lost in what they had to say to each other. We were drenched in sweat; even Viv was. My legs wanted to shake, the while we stood with our born-men forgetting us and so many strange creatures—a few were beautiful, but most were fierce—looking at us and wondering.

Dela shed her pack and dropped that with the helmet, and Griffin, who was dressed in clothes he must have gotten here—blue and green, they were, and not at all like ours—

Griffin drew her over to a rocky place that thrust up out of
the soil amid plants like vines that covered what must be
decking under our feet. Among the rocks stranger growth had
taken hold in soil heaped up about them. He gave her that
mossy place to sit, and sat down himself, holding her gloved
hands.

And Lance—he stood watching this, and finally gathered
more courage than any of us, and walked up to them and
knelt down there. So we all drifted closer. Griffin bent and
hugged Lance against him, a great fierce hug that warmed us
all and I think near broke Lance's heart.

"It's all right," Griffin said, looking worn and with tears
running down his face. And to Modred: "You were right."

"Yes, sir," Modred said, in that way of his. "I knew I
was."

We settled there, too tired to do more than that, and listened.

"I thought I was dead," Griffin said, "when they brought
me through the doors and took the helmet off. But it's what
you see here—I wanted to go back then and bring you here,
but I couldn't make them understand. Or trust me if they
did."

"They came through the ship," Dela said. "Modred saw."

"I think they went right on going," Modred said, "into the
tubes, after what lives there. What that is, I had no chance to
see. But they meant to stop it, and I think they have."

"We're safe," Griffin said, and took Dela's hand. "We can
rest here. Like the others."

A creature came to us—one so pale and delicate it seemed
more spirit than substance—and brought a flask of something
clear and a bit of what could only be bread. It cheered us im-
measurably, the more that it was pure water, clean and cold
and food that spoke worlds of likeness between us and these.
We were near and sibs to whatever creatures drank water and
breathed this air; our skins could touch; our could look
at other eyes without a faceplate between. We smiled, we
laughed, we cried, even we.

And then we shed the suits which were our last protection.
For Percy, we gave him all the ease we could, binding up his
arm, giving him what help we carried in our kits, so that he
had relief from pain. And after, one by one, we settled down
ourselves to sleep, absolutely undone. Griffin watched over

us, his arms about our lady, who slept against him. And creatures watched us strange as any heraldic beasts of our dream, but wise-eyed and armed and patient.

We thought we should never see the *Maid* again . . . but after what might have been two days, they opened up that great lock and showed us through, suitless themselves, so we knew it was safe.

And we went where they guided us, to visit our damaged home. They had sealed up the holes in the upper decks. It was all oxygen again.

But after some few days my lady missed the green wide expanses. So we came back to the huge lock bringing our baggage and whatever we could carry. And they opened for us—I think expected us, having come that way themselves.

It was not the last trip. They gave us stone, stones that like the soil were the fragments of wandering asteroids, and we understood, because there were all sorts of shelters if one wandered about the place. It was surely the strangest of human houses that we made, a simple place at first, a room for Griffin and my lady, with huge open windows, because the weather never varied and there was nothing there to fear. We carried the great dining table out when we had made another room, and set the banners there; there was the crystal and the fine plates. We dined together, and learned all manner of things grew here good to eat—of what source we only guessed, that some ships had brought plants in, some for food and some for air and more perhaps exotic things that were only beautiful.

And we became a wonder, having all kinds of visitors, some horrific and some very shy and beautiful. With some we learned to speak, or to make signs.

They came in a kind of respect. I think it was the banners, the bright brave colors, the shining crystal and the lovely things my lady Dela brought from the *Maid*. They took Griffin and my lady for very important, because we did; and because—in some strange fashion they loved the color we had brought.

So we settled there.

And lived.

Time . . . is different here. The Captain is very old . . .

no one knows how old, perhaps not even he. But we don't age.

And we fight his war, whenever he has need: Griffin and Lancelot and Gawain and Lynn . . . they've gotten very wise, and the Captain calls on them when it's a question of some ship in our sector—because more come. Our voyage is forever, and while the builders round our rim seldom win a ship, they always try. Like with us. They're methane-breathers; a plague; a determined folk . . . oh, very dangerous; but our air would kill them, so it's only ships they try, ships and sometimes great and terrible battles in methane sectors of the wheel where they can break through. And once there was a great battle, where all of us were called who could go—in our suits, and armed with terrible weapons.

There might be such again. We know.

But the time passes, and we gather others, who come whenever Griffin calls.

And we . . . we come, at such time: Modred from his berth on the *Maid*, where he spends endless time in talking with all sorts of living things and devising new ideas; and Vivien keeps him company, making meticulous records and accounts.

Percivale has a place up in the heights of the curve. We see him least of all; but very old and wise creatures visit him to talk philosophy, and when he comes to visit us his voice is quiet and makes one very warm.

And Gawain and Lynette—they travel about the land, even into the strange passages that lead elsewhere, so of all of us they have seen most and come with the strangest tales to tell.

And Lance—

"I love them both," he said once and long ago. And so he left the hall where Dela and Griffin lived, first of all to leave.

And that was the worst pain of any I had ever had.

"Where's Lance?" my lady asked that next day; and I was afraid for him. I ran.

But Griffin found me, all the same, there back of the house, where I thought that I was hidden.

"Where's Lance?" he said.

"He went away," I said, just that. But Griffin had always had a way of looking through me.

"Why?"

"For love," I said, which was a word so strange for me to be saying I was terrified. But it was so. It was nothing else but that.

"He shouldn't be alone," Griffin said. "Elaine—can you find him?"

"Yes," I said.

And he: "Go where you have to go."

So it was not so much trouble to track one of us, when every creature everywhere knew us. And I found Lance sitting on the shore of that huge lake which lies central to our world . . . itself a strange place and full of thinking creatures.

"Elaine," he said.

"They sent me," I said to him. And he made a place for me beside him.

So we live, Lance and I, in a tower on that shore, a long time in the building, but of time we have no end.

And from one window we look out on that vast lake; and from the other we look toward our Camelot.

Whether we dream, still falling forever, or whether the dream has shaped itself about us, we love . . . at least we dream we do.

And whenever the call goes out, echoing clear and brazen through the air, we take up our arms again and go.

DAW

SCIENCE FICTION MASTERWORKS FROM
THE INCOMPARABLE
C.J. CHERRYH

The Chanur Series
THE PRIDE OF CHANUR (UE2181—$3.50)
CHANUR'S VENTURE (UE2183—$3.50)
THE KIF STRIKE BACK (UE2184—$3.50)
CHANUR'S HOMECOMING (UE2177—$3.95)

The Union-Alliance Novels
DOWNBELOW STATION (UE1987—$3.50)
MERCHANTER'S LUCK (UE2139—$3.50)
FORTY THOUSAND IN GEHENNA (UE1952—$3.50)
VOYAGER IN NIGHT (UE2107—$2.95)

The Morgaine Novels
GATE OF IVREL (BOOK 1) (UE1956—$2.50)
WELL OF SHIUAN (BOOK 2) (UE1986—$2.95)
FIRES OF AZEROTH (BOOK 3) (UE1925—$2.50)

The Faded Sun Novels
THE FADED SUN: KESRITH (BOOK 1) (UE1960—$3.50)
THE FADED SUN: SHON'JIR (BOOK 2) (UE1889—$2.95)
THE FADED SUN: KUTATH (BOOK 3) (UE2133—$2.95)
